A Girl and a Dolphin

To Caroline and Patrick

A Girl and a Dolphin

Patrick O'Sullivan

WOLFHOUND PRESS

First published 1994 by
WOLFHOUND PRSS Ltd
68 Mountjoy Square
Dublin 1

Wolfhound Press receives financial assistance from the Arts Council/An
Chomhairle Ealaíon, Dublin.

British Library Cataloguing in Publication Data
A catalogue record for this book is available from the British Library.

ISBN 0-86327-426-9

Cover illustration: Katharine White
Cover design: Joe Gervin
Typesetting: Wolfhound Press
Printed by the Guernsey Press Co Ltd, Guernsey, Channel Isles.

CHAPTER ONE

A map of Kerry shows the village and townland of Claddaheen occupying a stretch of heavily indented coastline. The picturesque village, with its brightly painted shops facing the waterfront, attracts a great many tourists in summertime. There are boats of every kind in the harbour — small fishing boats, trawlers and tourist boats to take the visitors out on pleasure trips. An old-fashioned clock tower, painted in deep sienna and white, graces the pier which is generally littered with nets, ropes and weighted lobster pots. Here too are freshly painted wooden seats and there is a pungent smell of tar in the air that mingles with the bracing salty smell of the sea.

Anna O'Shea lived not in the village but in a farmhouse a little distance from it. Anna was a lover of country things; ever since she could walk she was always fascinated by the ways of nature, and the farmyard was a place of wonder for her. She enjoyed helping her mother to feed the hens or listening to her father sing as he milked the black Kerry cows.

In springtime there was the joy of watching the fluffy chicks emerge from the eggs beneath the brooding hen; in summer the blue-black swallows sometimes swept gaily in and out of the cowhouse. She often wondered about the swallows — what wonderful sights they must have seen on their long, long journey to Ireland.

An only child, she spent much of her time on her own and she liked it that way, wandering through the meadows or the damp rushy places, the silken swish of long grasses against her legs. She had come to know where the meadow pipits nested, where the moorhens swam in greeny ponds, where the goldfinch fed in thistle patches, where the water mint grew in clumps. Her father smiled when he saw her running through the fields or lazing beneath an overhanging tangle of deeply scented honeysuckle, her long blonde hair flowing loose about her shoulders, her bright blue eyes brighter still in summertime. She learned to swim too and took great delight in swimming in a sheltered cove almost directly beneath the farmhouse which nestled comfortably on the hillside above.

Anna was eleven and the secret cove was still one of her favourite places for it was partially hidden from view and no tourist strayed onto it. Her father had with some reluctance bought her a snorkel which allowed her to breathe while face down on the surface of the water. Sometimes she snorkelled down through the shimmering blue and the water closed over her for a few moments. She loved its cool swell about her body and for those few precious moments she felt she could imagine what it was like to be a fish. The sea in the cove was always blue or blue-green, sandy cliffs rising all around, gulls or puffins flying past overhead, silver sprats sometimes dangling from their bills. The puffins were her favourites — they had black backs, white bellies, grey faces and fabulously coloured bills. There was a colony of puffins on the island which rose up sharp and angular some three to four miles out from the coast; here they nested in tunnels which they burrowed themselves or which they borrowed from unsuspecting rabbits or shearwaters. Anna had often visited the island with her father and he had told her that the puffins generally laid one single egg which soon became covered with dust. The island was a great attraction, not only for those with a special interest in birds but also for those who liked to wander amongst old ruins and abbeys, for there was an old abbey on the island. It was a very fine abbey, their teacher said, but Anna was more interested in the puffins and the shearwaters, the rabbits and the rocky slopes that were sometimes embellished with colourful clumps of vivid sea pink.

Her father took her lobster fishing too, giving her a turn at the oars now and then. It was great fun hauling in the buoys, each of which was attached to a string of pots. Then the lobsters clattered about in the pots on the floor of the boat. Sometimes she was tempted to wish that the pots might be empty, as she did not like to see the lobsters trapped. But she knew that her father's small farm was hilly and marshy and the family could not survive without the extra money that came from the fish. It was the view from the boat that Anna enjoyed most of all. In one direction there was the village and the coastline while far away in the other direction was the island and its birds. Her father fished for herring and salmon too but only very rarely did Anna go on such fishing trips.

One sunny Saturday at the end of May Anna cycled down to the cove as usual. The hedgerows were white with hawthorn blossoms and sunlight danced on the water. She brought with her a lobster pot, and had a rope and a buoy ready on the strand. She and her father had had a friendly bet, Anna betting that there would be a lobster in the pot within three days, her father betting that there would not. A lobster had never been caught in the cove below the house, he told her, and if his father were alive he would tell her the very same thing. Anna was not discouraged, however, and so when she had put on her swimsuit she hurried into the water, adjusting the snorkel on her head. The water felt cold at first and sent shivers racing through her body. Anna was very keen to select just the right place for the lobster pot and eventually decided on a spot close to one of the headlands jutting out into the tide. Then she took some time to settle the pot on the end of the line, swimming down and down again to do this to her satisfaction before she would let the pot free from her grasp. It was while she was tending to the lobster pot in this way that she caught a fleeting glimpse of a huge grey mass sweeping past her. Alarmed, she shot to the surface. What she had seen was blurred and indistinct but one ominous feature had registered clearly in her mind — the huge dorsal fin surging through the water. A shark! A shark! The words pounded in her brain. Sharks were sometimes seen further out at sea during the summer time — porbeagle sharks her father called them — and now one of them had strayed into her secret cove.

Anna was numb with fear. It was the first time she had ever felt afraid in the water in her life. She swam towards the rocky headland which was nearer than the strand, desperately trying to make swift rhythmic strokes with her hands and vigorously kicking her legs. Suddenly the great black fin became visible again, cutting through the water a little distance from her. Next moment Anna's heart leapt with relief and joy. The massive grey creature that had whizzed past her was not a shark at all but a dolphin, for now it had broken the surface and that distinctive bottle-nosed head was unmistakable. Anna could scarcely believe her eyes.

Fabulous! fabulous! a wild dolphin, and here in her secret place!

The girl remained motionless in the water for some time, watching the progress of the newcomer. He did not leap or somersault through the air for at first he seemed determined to investigate the lobster pot and the line, disappearing under the water only to resurface elsewhere. He seemed almost elated by his intriguing discovery as he surveyed the pot now from one angle, now from another. Had he heard the swish of the line in the water, Anna wondered, or the heavy splash of the aluminium buoy? Her father would be so excited when he heard the news.

How beautifully, effortlessly the dolphin curled and curved and what a massive size he seemed to be. These were just impressions though, for the dolphin moved with such incredible speed and agility, veering playfully now to the left and now to the right, that it was impossible to get a close-up view of him. And yet the impression was one of majesty and power, of a creature that was master in his own kingdom but who had an overwhelming almost insatiable curiosity as he studied the lobster pot and the line from every conceivable angle.

At first Anna succumbed to such a feeling of wonder and amazement that she remained perfectly still in the water. Despite the massive size of the dolphin, she felt not the slightest hint of fear. There were gulls in the sky overhead but she did not hear their raucous cries. Only when it seemed that the newcomer had finished his inspection of the lobster pot; only when it seemed that he was preparing to head out to sea again, only then did the girl snorkel down into the greeny-blue once more. If only she could get a good look at his face! The dolphin swam towards her and as he drew near he made a spectacular leap into the air, leaving an arch of silver spray dripping in his wake. Anna had seen dolphins on television and her father had told her stories of the dolphin that had supposedly been seen very far out near the island years ago, but nothing could compare with the joy of seeing a real live dolphin close at hand. Down came the dolphin again crashing and splashing through the water, myriads of bubbles and ripples swirling all around. Then came a boisterous downward curve and an energetic roll as he rose nearer the surface again. Anna could see him a little more clearly now. His body was lissome and streamlined, and how wonderfully he could propel himself upwards or downwards to the right or to the left with that magnificent tail which he swished up and down with such purpose and power. Seconds later he leapt from the water again, a spectacular leap of uninhibited joy and exuberance, the sunlight glinting in his eyes. When he plunged through the surface once more he came closer, much closer to the girl than he had been before.

This was the most magical experience of Anna's life. She was side by side with a wild dolphin in her secret place. She longed to reach out her hand and touch him, caress him, but she was afraid that she might frighten him away with such a gesture, so she continued to swim and snorkel, the dolphin whizzing past her one moment, only to turn and sweep past in the other direction seconds later. He was just as curious about her as she was about him — his sense of excitement was almost as palpable as her own. What did he think of this strange creature in the water beside him? Had he ever come this close to a human before?

He seemed particularly intrigued by her legs for he moved closer to them than to any other part of her body. Maybe he imagined them as curiously elongated tails which, however, did not seem very well adapted for movement in the water.

How she wished that he would hang motionless in the

water for a moment or two so that she might get a clearer image of him, but he did not do so. He was just as intense, just as excited at the novelty of this chance encounter as she was. He made another fantastic leap, a silver arch of spray again rising high behind him, the sweeping movement of his tail playfully cutting the air. Then the bottle-nose came through the greeny-blue water once more. Anna snorkelled down and rose to the surface again. There were showers of bubbles all around when the graceful arch of the back and the vigorous stroke of the tail disappeared beneath the water. The dolphin's elation was infectious for his companion had never felt such wild emotion before.

When at last the dolphin moved away from her she made no attempt to entice him to stay any longer for he was a creature of the deep, wild and free, and it was that freedom to do as he pleased that made him so endearing, so special. Yet she could not resist calling after him, 'Come back again, come back again.' When he had swum a good distance from her Anna returned to the shore. Her meeting with the dolphin had lasted only a few moments but those were magical moments, moments of mystery and enchantment that she would never forget. And now there was one wish in her heart which overwhelmed all others and that was that the dolphin would return soon again.

When she had dressed she cycled furiously along the winding road, eager to share her news. She had quite forgotten the lobster pot and the bet with her father. She could think only of the dolphin — her dolphin — he must have a name, but what? She thought as urgently as she could. He seemed to cut through the water so effortlessly she would call him Cutty. Yes, Cutty was a good name, she assured herself with satisfaction, thrusting the bicycle against the stone wall that fronted the flower garden.

She dashed along the garden pathway, but when she came in her father was sitting at the table, looking pale and shaken. Anna asked him what was wrong, still gasping to catch her breath.

'Donal Mike! That's what's wrong,' her father answered wearily. Donal Mike was the local name given to Donal Jones. His father owned the largest guesthouse in the village as well as a number of boats, employing men during the summer to take tourists on pleasure trips. Donal spent a good deal of his time wind-surfing or water-skiing or whizzing around in his speed boat. 'We had a narrow escape, your Uncle Tadhg and me,' he explained. 'We were coming around by Carraig-narone when Donal almost ploughed straight into us with his fibreglass contraption — speeding like the wind as always.'

Anna sat and listened. She was so impatient, desperately wanting to tell her mother and father about her encounter with the dolphin but also anxious to hear her father's story, and to satisfy herself that he had not been hurt. 'He came within inches of us. I thought we were going to be capsized but it was the will of God that he managed to veer suddenly to the right and there was no damage done.'

'Are you sure you're all right, Dad?' Anna asked moving closer to him. He gave her a reassuring nod and smile, placing his arm about her waist and hugging her warmly.

'You should tell his father,' Anna's mother said.

'A lot of good that would do,' Anna's father replied. 'Jones takes no notice of what his son does. In fact he seems quite proud of Donal's escapades — he'd rather have a son with spirit than a wimp.'

'Spirit is one thing,' the woman went on, 'but he must realise that Donal is not only a danger to himself but other people too.'

'Well, if he does, he's keeping very quiet about it,' her

husband smiled. 'Jones used to like to think of himself as a hard man in his own day, they say, and I suppose he thinks it's only natural that Donal should behave the way he does. Besides, Donal is harmless enough most of the time.'

Anna could restrain herself no longer. With a rush of excitement and enthusiasm she told her parents about the dolphin. Her father listened intently, his dark blue eyes brightening with interest. 'A dolphin in the cove,' he repeated incredulously.

'Yes, yes,' his daughter assured him, recounting everything that had happened in minute detail. They could sense the tingling excitement in her voice. Anna told of how the dolphin had leapt and dived, creating magical rainbows of spray, the bubbles winking all around.

No one in the village had mentioned sighting a dolphin, her father said, and he would surely have heard it if there had been such a sighting. All Anna could think of now was would the dolphin come again and if he did how long could his presence in the area remain a secret? Not for long, her father assured her, for his antics were sure to attract attention, but maybe long enough for Anna to get to know him better.

After supper, when they had finished milking they went down to the strand to see if they could catch another glimpse of him. Anna peered out to sea, hoping against hope that her new-found friend would reveal himself by leaping high into the air, but there was no sign of him. Nor did the dolphin come the next day, Sunday, and so it was with mixed feelings of joy and uncertainty that Anna made her way to school on Monday morning. There was the joy of remembering with delight that she really had spent those precious moments with Cutty in the water but there was the nagging uncertainty too that she might never see him again.

CHAPTER TWO

The days that followed were warm and sunny and Anna was scarcely home from school when she cycled down to the strand, full of anticipation and expectancy. There was no sign of Cutty on Monday or Tuesday and she was keenly disappointed. She consoled herself, however, by beginning what she called her 'dolphin diary' — a secret diary in which she would write of all her experiences with the dolphin. There was such happiness even in remembering that first magical encounter with Cutty in the cove. She would never forget those first explosive leaps of his into the air, his skin so smooth, his body so streamlined and the exhilaration with which he soared and dived. He seemed so full of the joys of life. As Anna penned her thoughts in a neat script in the diary she was still unsure whether Cutty would return. Sometimes she moved to her bedroom window and looked towards her secret place — which was partially hidden from view — desperately hoping that she would see him there, the powerful upward and downward strokes of his tail propelling him through the water.

On Wednesday she found a book about wildlife in the school library and read that dolphins were fascinated by sound. That gave her an idea. She would try to call Cutty to her. After school she went for a swim in the chilly water of the cove. When she had moved some distance from the shore she took the line from which she had suspended four small aluminium sweet-tin lids and shook it vigorously beneath the water so that the lids clattered together and the metallic clang reverberated through the brine. At first it seemed as if her less than scientific experiment would not work; either Cutty did not hear the clanging of the lids or if he did he was choosing to ignore it. But it was not long before Anna's heart leapt, for there came sweeping towards her a jutting beak and dome-shaped head.

She scarcely noticed the cold now as she shook the line; still the clatter of the lids sent sound waves throbbing through the water. Anna marvelled again at the dolphin's speed and strength. When he came nearer she adjusted the snorkel on her head and sank beneath the surface and this time he came much closer than before. Clearly the clanging of the lids attracted him. Cutty rolled and curled for a few moments before moving in for a more minute investigation of the lids. He began to prod them playfully with his massive beak and it was while he was absorbed in this game of prodding — for everything seemed to be a game to Cutty — that the girl could fully appreciate his enormous size. Her heart was pounding.

Images under water were sometimes distorted, making things look larger than they were, but Cutty was really huge; he must be ten to twelve feet long. The lids flashed and shimmered in the sunlight and yet Anna knew that it was not the flashing light but the clang of metal against metal that intrigued the dolphin. Cutty was looking towards her now and this was her first real chance to study his face. His most distinctive features were the small bright eyes and the grinning lips. Those beautiful eyes seemed so warm and intelligent, so curious and mischievous too. They told her more than words ever could for they seemed to say that Cutty was not only master of his environment but also sensitive to everything around him.

The dolphin's lips seemed to be set in a permanent smile but she caught a glimpse of his finely edged teeth and yet did not feel afraid. There was no sensation of fear — only of elation, for the closeness of the dolphin made her feel special, and filled her with heart-felt wonder.

When Anna surfaced again Cutty began to swim in arches about her. He was clearly happy to see her again. She hoped he would leap from the water and she was not disappointed for in a moment he flung himself high with an explosive burst of energy and vigour. Anna observed his antics with rapt emotions for though Cutty's leaps and somersaults were powerful and strong, they were also masterfully graceful and poised. Cutty was so self-possessed, so dignified, so composed and it seemed to please him that his breath-taking displays were appreciated by his new-found friend.

'Oh Cutty, you're beautiful,' Anna said spontaneously as if trying to translate her thoughts into words, 'the most beautiful fellow I've ever seen. We'll be friends, won't we?'

Maybe Cutty could not understand her words but he could sense the friendliness in her voice — and she really needed a friend for though she liked most of those in her class at school she had formed no special bond with any of them — and the fabulous Cutty would be the most magical friend anyone could ever have. When Cutty swam round and round he generally kept his mouth submerged beneath the water even when the rest of his head broke the surface, so it was clear that he did not use his mouth for breathing. As she had read in the library book, his nostrils were located on top of his head in a little opening called the blowhole and when he surfaced the blowhole opened and there came forth a sudden blast of air. One of the most remarkable things about him was his tail, for it was not set vertically like a fish's tail, the top pointing towards the surface, rather it was horizontal with the surface of the water and was pumping upwards and downwards with incredible ease. This horizontal setting of the tail seemed to allow him to dive and surface at will as he came to the surface to breathe, the blowhole being held firmly closed when he sank beneath the water.

Again there was the temptation to reach out and touch him, to stroke the dripping smoothness of his skin, and this time Anna reached out her hand, but when she did Cutty moved suddenly to the right and swam away. It was clear that the notion of being stroked did not appeal to him; his sudden withdrawal seemed to be telling her that he was the master in this element and he would decide when the time was right for touching. The girl felt a strange kind of guilt. It was as if she had offended him in some way, violated his freedom.

If the winsome Cutty had been offended he did not remain so for very long for he soon returned and swam about her. Anna talked to him again. 'I wouldn't hurt you, Cutty. I just wanted to touch you, but I won't if you'd rather not. Can I just look at you?'

He seemed to agree, for he gave yet another boisterous leap. As she watched, he rolled and somersaulted high in the air and then went diving down, cutting the water in two, magical ripples of spume and frothy bubbles swirling in his wake.

Anna had much to write in her dolphin diary that night

and she was sure that a bond was forming between herself and Cutty. Of course it was only a matter of time before someone else spotted him but even then he would still be her dolphin in a very special way for she had been the first human he had come to know. She hoped that he would never become a plaything for the amusement of humans. If he made people happy that was fine as long as he was doing what he pleased and did not have to follow the dictates of a trainer. And yet it was her dearest wish that Cutty would remain her secret for a little while longer.

On Thursday Cutty did not come, but on Friday Anna had an idea. Cutty was obviously interested in sound. Would he come to her if she played her tin whistle near the water? She would try. She had no great gift for the tin whistle, but the dolphin would probably be less critical than her music teacher. That evening she climbed out to a rock and sat with her feet in the water, playing all the tunes she knew. At last her patience was rewarded and the big black dorsal fin came sweeping towards her once more.

Her heart leapt again; her senses were overwhelmed with a wild kind of emotion that only came upon her when Cutty was near for his presence — grey in the water, flashing silver in the air — seemed to radiate happiness all around. Nearer and nearer he came. Still Anna played on the tin whistle. When he came a little distance from her, Cutty popped up his head and hung vertically motionless in the water as if listening intently to the music. She could see the sunlight sparkle in his small bright eyes; he was listening all right, she was sure of that, and he liked what he heard. Then he shook his head from side to side and made a kind of chattering sound before turning away to swim once more. Silver droplets like diamonds flew whenever he rose high into the air. There was a kind of gay abandon in those spectacular leaps; it seemed as if he were flinging himself, hurling himself from the water, completely indifferent to everything but the thrill of the moment, his entire being invigorated not only by the sun and the sea but also by the nearness of the girl and her music. Cutty really did have an ear for music, Anna told herself, as he dived and curled and rolled beneath the water only to surface once more.

Anna's parents watched from the strand. They had never seen their daughter so wildly excited about anything. It was as if her encounter with the dolphin had touched some chord deep within her spirit.

As she wrote in her diary that night Anna wondered how she might tempt her new-found friend to allow her to touch him and stroke him. He seemed curiously resistant to the notion of a human coming in contact with his skin. She was already beginning to form some impression of his character — he was inquisitive, mischievous, boisterous one moment, gentle the next. Above all, he seemed to have an innate sense of fun for not only did he take great pleasure in arching through the air like a silver rainbow, he seemed to derive a double pleasure from the knowledge that he was giving an exhibition for the amusement of his human companion. One of Cutty's greatest attractions however was that in reality she knew very little about him. This imbued him with a kind of mystery for he was totally different to a favourite cat or dog. Anna did not know where he had been born or what adventures he experienced before seeking out the seclusion of the long narrow cove. There was an expression of concentration on the girl's face as she wrote about her latest encounter with the dolphin. She had been tempted to shout with ecstasy when Cutty had hurled himself spectacularly into the air — now she half regretted that she had not done so for Cutty would surely have appreciated such adulation.

Before she went to bed Anna went downstairs and had a cup of cocoa with her father and mother in the living room. Her father had had no further close encounters with Donal Jones and his speedboat, for Donal and his friend Tom had been too busy diving. They were trying to locate the wreck of a Spanish galleon which had been part of the Spanish Armada in 1588 and which, according to tradition, had foundered in a storm off the coast of Claddaheen. They had made a number of similar attempts the previous summer but their efforts had all been in vain. Nobody really knew for certain if the *San Juan* had come anywhere near the coast of Claddaheen and even if it had, nobody had the slightest indication of the general area in which it might have gone down.

'Your uncle Tadhg thinks such diving isn't right at all,' Anna's father mused.

'Why?' the girl asked with some surprise.

'No good comes from digging into the past, he says,' her father replied, 'no good from disturbing the bones of long dead sailors.' He paused and smiled. 'Not much chance of that though. Tom tried to do a bit of research but came up with very little, so himself and Donal are taking pot luck — diving here there and everywhere at random.'

'I'm surprised they've started to search for the wreck again,' Anna's mother said. 'Donal is the kind who gets very excited about something one day and has completely forgotten about it two days later.'

'He'd have forgotten about the wreck too if Eamonn King and some of the lads hadn't started ribbing him about it in the pub the other night,' Anna's father explained. 'Eamonn was getting on at him about the wild promises he was making this time last year.'

'What promises?' Anna asked, stroking the cat on her lap.

'Oh, boasting about how he'd have Spanish coins to show

the tourists and stuff. Eamonn of course is a bit of a weasel but most of the boys meant no harm. Donal got really rattled though.'

'I'm not surprised Tadhg doesn't approve,' said Anna's mother. 'Sure he wouldn't even go fishing if he met a red-haired woman on the road.'

'A rabbit in a field is another thing he doesn't like to see when we're on our way down to the pier,' her husband agreed.

Anna did not like her uncle Tadhg too much. He could be quite moody at times, and the weasel Eamonn was a frequent visitor at his house. It was very difficult to please him. He was always laying down the law about boats and nets and lobster pots for her father but her father didn't seem to mind. Tadhg was never as happy as when he was finding fault with something or someone, her father said. Anna sometimes wondered how Mella put up with him. Mella was in her class at school. She was not Tadhg's daughter but his stepdaughter. He had married her mother just a year ago. Mella's father had been drowned while fishing one rainswept night in March some years before and one of those who had been with him in the boat at the time was the man who was now married to her mother — a cruel twist of destiny. Anna felt sorry for Mella. She realised just how lucky she was to have a father and a mother whom she could love with all her heart, and who returned that love with the same depth of feeling.

Cutty came to the cove again and again in the days that followed. Each time he came Anna played on the tin whistle for him before diving into the water to join him. Often he really did play games with her; he circled about her before surging towards her at great speed only to veer suddenly to the right or to the left at the last moment. There was never any fear when he came sweeping towards her through the

21

water — only feelings of elation and exhilaration. The seemingly effortless way in which he manoeuvred his body at great speed never ceased to fill her with awe. The flukes of the massive tail provided the propulsion, while the flippers provided the direction. Sometimes he indulged in a game of hide and seek, for Anna had often come to the conclusion that he had deserted her when suddenly he reappeared, rising from the dark green waters below or cruising past her with mischievous delight. It was as if he knew what she was thinking, as if he knew that she thought he had vanished. Sometimes he seemed baffled by her incompetence in the water, perhaps wondering why she could not roll and dive, curl and somersault beneath the water as he did with such ease. The creature with the two long tails could make nice sounds, he must have told himself, but she was not the best when it came to under-water frolics. Many of those frolics were not without purpose for it seemed as if he were tempting her to put on her snorkel and come down with him and play. It was as if he were speaking to her with his body. 'Look, look at me. I'm having fun. Come and join me,' was what he seemed to say and it was very difficult to resist an invitation to take part in such high-spirited games.

And yet despite this apparent closeness it seemed to Anna that Cutty was determined to maintain a certain distance from her. Whenever she made any movement to reach out and touch him he immediately sped away or launched himself high into the air. Anna sensed that this response was deliberate, for the graceful mysterious creature from the deep seemed to think that any direct contact with the girl might somehow diminish his freedom. And yet Anna hoped that as the bond between them deepened she might yet be given the privilege of touching his skin with her hand. That would surely be a magical sensation.

CHAPTER THREE

It was a grey misty June day. On a white-hulled boat, motion-less in the water, Donal Jones and his friend Tom were getting themselves ready for the dive. The brown-eyed Donal strug-gled to adjust the metal cylinder of his breathing apparatus on his back. His eyes were filled with anticipation. His friend Tom who was more methodical and meticulous about his diving gear was also ready at last, positioning the mouthpiece of the oxygen regulator. Seconds later they dived into the grey-green haze and the water closed over them. A line suspended from the port side of the stationary boat would help them to relocate their craft. Donal was very excited. He was sure he had seen very old timbers on the ocean floor the previous day but he'd had to surface because visibility had been terrible and he had been running low on oxygen. Could those old timbers be part of the wreck of the *San Juan*? If they were they had stumbled upon them quite by accident for they'd had no plan or method — much to Tom's annoyance — listening only to the stories of some of the older residents of Claddaheen.

Visibility was still not great but at least it was better than the day before. The sea bed was littered with boulders and rocks, not a few of which reared their heads dangerously close to the surface. Crayfish and crabs scuttled here and there between them, and herring swam past. It was the rocks that gave Donal hope. It was surely one of the likeliest sites they had explored to date for it seemed perfectly plausible that the great galleon might have gone to her doom when the hull had struck the underwater edge of these menacingly jagged rocks. He could imagine the terrible crash, sea water flooding in and doomed sailors struggling in the water.

The divers moved apart for a few moments. The water was still and green, disturbed only by the bubbles from their oxygen masks as they held their gaze firmly on the ocean floor. This had to be the area where he had glimpsed the timbers, Donal told himself; they would have marked the spot if they'd had a buoy in the boat. The water was pleasantly cool but as always the images were curiously distorted at times and they could never see very far. Nobody had very much confidence in Donal; most of the people of Claddaheen thought he was likeable enough but wild and reckless. Cruising at high speed whether on land or at sea seemed to be his only goal in life, for if he wasn't in his father's speedboat he was whizzing along the road in his flashy sports car. Most of the teenagers were jealous of him. The only work he ever seemed to do was to take tourists out on pleasure trips during the summertime, and he did not even do that on a regular basis for his father owned a number of currach-type boats fitted with outboard motors and he employed men to ferry the tourists back and forth to the island and around the harbour. He seemed invigorated by the wind and the waves whenever he went water skiing, the spray dripping from his wavy auburn hair, but even his father seemed to have come to accept that his son did not have the commitment and the dedication to see any project through to the end. Diving for the wreck of the *San Juan* was just another of his hare-brained fads — a fad which he had entirely forgotten for nine months or more. While Donal enjoyed his wild reputation he desperately wanted to prove — to others and to himself — that he really would persevere until something was achieved.

Soon, very soon, his eyes fell upon an unforgettable sight. There beneath him on the stony ocean floor was an enormous timber pole. His heart pounded in the eerie underwater stillness. He dived still lower to investigate. Could it be one of the mast poles of the ill-fated Spanish galleon? Tom came and joined him. The gigantic pole did appear to be very old. It was green and rotting in parts. The divers looked at each other with mounting excitement. Though they had no definite proof they sensed that they were very close to finding the wreck that had eluded them for so long. They explored the area adjacent to the pole in some detail but if there were any further clues here they could not find them and so they decided to move on, hoping that further investigations would bring rewards. And they were not disappointed, for it was not long before they came upon the timbers that Donal had glimpsed the previous day: massive timbers littered and strewn about the floor of the ocean. They had surely formed the hull of some once-proud ship, but which ship? The planks seemed to be scattered over a wide area and like the giant pole they too gave the impression that they were centuries old. Donal had never felt such tingling excitement in his life as he moved from one plank to another. This must surely be the grave of the *San Juan*. Already he was coming to a decision: if this really was the wreck of the Spanish galleon they must do everything in their power to keep the location a secret until they had explored it fully.

His gaze was distracted by a crayfish for a moment and it was then that he caught a glimpse of something embedded amongst the stones. He moved towards it and struggled to release it with his hands. It appeared to be a tiny scrap of metal but he could not get it free. He reached down and withdrew his diving knife from the holder strapped to the calf of his leg and with it he began to gently prize the tiny metal object free. Though he was tempted to jerk the blade now and then he did not do so lest he might damage his precious find, for whatever it was it might present him with some clue as to the identity of the wreck. Slowly, slowly he worked around the little piece of metal. When at last he held it in his hand it seemed totally insignificant but then his pulse began to throb again when he observed that there were some letters inscribed in the metal.

Though they explored amongst the planks for quite some time, the tiny scrap of metal which appeared to be a medal or badge of some kind was the only find they made — and yet it was with some elation that they returned to the boat, having made careful note of the precise location of the wreck. As they approached the boat they observed that at times it seemed to rock curiously from side to side, though there was no wind at all. But there was no real mystery here for Cutty the dolphin was curling and curving round about it, sometimes taking the notion to roll on his back and rub his belly against the keel, from which he seemed to derive immense pleasure. By now Cutty's arrival in Claddaheen was a matter of common knowledge for he had been spotted making exuberant leaps high in the air and he seemed to have established some kind of territory for himself at the mouth of the harbour. Cutty had great fun accompanying the fishing boats in and out of the harbour, sometimes escorting them to their fishing grounds. He was a great source of amusement and delight for most people and there were those who said he would do wonders for the tourist trade. Donal's father for one was expecting a much busier season than usual for Cutty had already made news in *The Kerryman* and it would surely not be long before he became the centre of attraction for the national media too. There was great talk in the village of how the dolphin sometimes liked to ride the bow waves of the boats; he was a great character, they said, for one of his great objectives in life appeared to be having fun.

Donal was not too keen on the dolphin now, however. He had followed their boat on more than one occasion and his aerial acrobatics were sure to attract attention to them — attention they clearly did not want now that they seemed to have stumbled on one of the greatest discoveries of their life. When they drew near to the boat, Cutty swam away from the keel, the flukes of his tail beating up and down and his black dorsal fin visible above the water.

'That dolphin could be a right nuisance,' Donal said when he clambered on board and deposited the metal fragment on the floor of the boat. The two friends began to remove their flippers and their wet suits.

'Ah he's a likeable rascal,' Tom replied cheerfully, rubbing his fingers through his dark curly hair. 'He seems to get bored easily, doesn't stay in the one place for long, and besides if anyone does see him near the boat they'll think we're just diving — they won't know we've found anything, will they?'

'Eamonn will be watching us like a hawk,' Donal retorted as he dried his legs. 'If he sees the dolphin he'll know we're spending a great deal of time in this one area — something we've never done up to now.'

'I know, we've been like a pair of wandering jackdaws,' Tom laughed but his friend was in a serious mood for once.

This was a serious matter; they might be on the verge of discovering a small fortune in gold and jewels and he was not having his chances ruined by a pesky dolphin. If the dolphin did not go and divert himself elsewhere there was sure to be trouble, he mused grimly, taking the medal in his hand and rubbing it gently with a clean cloth. The metal, though not in very good condition, appeared to be silver and the letters were AMGP. Tom watched intently as the letters became more and more distinct. What did they represent?

Tom spent most of that afternoon rummaging through books in the library and finally came up with the answer. The letters stood for 'Ave Maria Gratia Plena,' the Latin for Hail Mary, Full of Grace. Many of the sails on the ships that had formed the Spanish Armada had borne that legend for the Armada had been very much a religious crusade and great quantities of medals of every kind had been presented to the sailors.

There was no doubt about it, the two friends concluded when they met later in the pub: they had found the wreck of the *San Juan.* Even more exciting had been the statement in one of the books that many of the Armada ships had been carrying vast quantities of money. It was like a dream come true, Donal told Tom as they then made their way along one of the narrow side streets. Sunlight was slanting against the windows of the brightly-coloured shops with their lovingly maintained timber fronts and their hanging baskets teeming with flowers. In one sense the guesthouse owner's son was bursting to tell some of the lads, apart from Eamonn, about their find — to let them see that he had made a nonsense of all their mocking guffaws — but he knew that Tom was right when he suggested that such a course of action would be self-defeating. They would simply have to keep the site a secret until they had explored it more fully. Tom talked about

the historical significance of the wreck — he was like that —
but Donal was merely worried that some more experienced
divers might move in like sharks and make off with the loot
when they themselves had done all the hard graft. Above all
they did not want some goody-goody expert coming down
from Dublin telling them to clear off because they didn't have
official permission in triplicate to investigate the wreck. But
would the dolphin prove to be a problem? Would he spoil all
their plans, Donal wondered. Of course, he wouldn't, Tom
assured him, but he did not seem convinced.

Cutty the dolphin was now the subject of many conversa-
tions in Claddaheen, but what most people did not know was
that he made time almost every day to visit a narrow cove a
little further up the coast from the village harbour. Anna now
had many entries in her diary, amongst them one describing
the first exciting moment when she had touched the beautiful
Cutty .... One calm bright evening Cutty came cruising towards her through the water and her heart was full of welcome for him. Though others had seen him and admired him
he was still in a very special sense her dolphin — not in the
sense of ownership but in the sense of deep abiding comrade-
ship. She played the tin whistle for him. 'Fáinne Geal an Lae'
was the tune she knew really well, and while she played, it
was always Cutty's custom to hang vertical in the tide, his
head above the water, his eyes shining with interest. He really
did appreciate her music for sometimes he shook his head
from side to side and grinned and chattered — this was his
way of applauding, Anna told herself — and then he plunged
and leapt about her with incredible agility. He was surely
saying he liked those musical sounds.

Then Anna produced the new paint brush she had brought
with her, a brush with velvet soft bristles. She held it at
arms length and stroked the dolphin's side with it. It was a

sensation that pleased him though at first it seemed to tickle him and make him skittish. Then he became gentle again and he did not move away as the girl had expected. Her eyes were filled with wonder as she gently stroked the bristles of the brush backwards and forwards against Cutty's skin, the dolphin remaining almost stationary beside her. She was learning new things about him every day. He really did seem to have a very sensitive sense of touch. She continued to stroke the skin with the brush for quite some time. Then she summoned the courage to put down the brush and to touch the smoothness of his skin with her fingers, recreating the same stroking movement that she had produced with the brush. Cutty turned his head and looked directly towards her. This felt different, he seemed to say, but it was not unpleasant.

Anna felt a surge of exhilaration when her fingers made contact with the shining skin. Cutty's skin was as soft as velvet and yet she could sense its robustness too. It was the silkiness of the skin as well as the streamlining of the body that gave her companion such speed and buoyancy in the water. She would never cease to be filled with admiration for his beauty, wonder at his great size and awe at his total mastery of the waves. Writing in her diary later, she struggled to find words to describe her feelings when her fingers first stroked his beautiful side, but this could not be translated into words, structured into sentences, restricted by commas and full stops. The closest she could come to describing it was to say that it reminded her of that wonderful feeling when she walked alone through grasses long and lush in the stillness of a scented twilight.

If stroking the dolphin's skin had been wonderful, how much more so was her experience some days later when she grasped his dorsal fin and held fast to it as Cutty sped through the green and blue of the cove. At first she was terrified that he might become too excited and lash her body with his tail or ram her with his massive beak to shake her off; or that he might leap suddenly and send her spinning through the air as helpless as a feather in the wind; or that he would race out to sea taking her with him. These were only passing fears, however, for Cutty preferred to curl and curve and arch and weave wonderful patterns in the water. Every fibre of Anna's being was focused on the task of holding on to the dorsal fin and holding her breath and yet she was acutely aware of the water sweeping and surging past her, the dolphin still cutting a trail of frothy spray as he cruised along. She was the luckiest girl in the world.

Sometimes it seemed as if Cutty meant to slow down but then there came another burst of acceleration and he swept Anna off again, water rushing and gushing all about her body. It was a magical ride and Cutty seemed to enjoy the experience as much as she did. It was as if he sensed how wonderful such a ride would be for a creature who seemed cumbersome and slow underwater. She felt as if she were completely weightless, as if the pull of gravity no longer exerted its influence on her.

One Saturday afternoon, Anna was sitting with her father in the fishing boat which was moving away from the pier at Claddaheen. The sky was blue and cloudless and Cutty was escorting a speedboat driven by a young man out to the mouth of the harbour, his leaping and diving as exuberant as ever. Moments later another speedboat came speeding towards the first from the opposite direction. Anna recognised the occupants of the second boat as Donal and Tom. Then both boats began to loop and curve and coil at high speed about the wide expanse of the harbour mouth, the blonde-haired driver of the first boat raising his hand and waving towards Donal and his companion. The boats zoomed round and round at incredible speed, their prows lifting from the water and seeming to skim the waves. The playful dolphin gambolled in and out between them. Anna observed the speeding boats with some anxiety. Cutty seemed unaware of any danger. The boats churned up the water, making it froth with foaming swells of spume. The two crafts were soon making figures of eight in the water, a buzz of elation coursing through Donal's body when the bows almost cut one another. The thrill of the speed and the danger made him tremble. Anna's expression became more and more tense. She clenched her fists. Seconds later her worst fears were realised when Cutty rose up suddenly from the green underwater world and the prow of a boat came sweeping down upon him. The blonde-haired boatman tried to swerve, but it was too late. The prow of the boat struck the silver-grey hump of the dolphin at high speed and sent him reeling with pain. 'Oh God, Cutty's been hit,' Anna shouted. There was anguish in her voice and agony in her eyes. She couldn't believe what had happened. How could they have been so reckless, so thoughtless?

Now the speedboats had come to a halt and the blonde-haired man jumped into the water in a state of flurried agitation to see if the dolphin had been badly hurt, to see if he could help in any way. He felt ashamed and guilty; he had not meant to hurt the dolphin, only to share its enthusiasm for speed and fun. But there was only an ominous patch of red blood in the water and no trace of the beautiful dolphin. The man clambered back dejectedly into the boat, sad and sickened by the sight of the blood. Donal and Tom were soon speeding back towards the shore; Tom felt very sad and even Donal had mixed feelings. Yes, the dolphin had been a nuisance and yes, he had expressed a wish that he would go and amuse himself elsewhere but now he regretted his words.

Anna's father slowed the boat and the girl's eyes filled with tears when she saw the blood in the water. She felt a sudden rush of rage against the careless boatmen.

'How could they? How could they?' she asked in disbelief, the tears blinding her eyes. Her father had no answers. She held her gaze on the blood. It looked so incongruous, so ugly in the sunlight. Tears flooded down her cheeks, and her father switched off the motor for a moment. He placed his arm around Anna. Cutty was a strong, resilient fellow he said: he would not give up without a fight and he had surely received only a gash in his flesh, perhaps a deep gash but even a deep gash would heal. Nature had ways of making things mend again. Anna tried to hear what her father was telling her. She hoped, how she hoped that the injury would heal but even if it did would the accident shatter the dolphin's confidence in humankind? Would he ever return to her secret cove again — and if he didn't how would she ever know if he had lived or died?

CHAPTER FOUR

June days were slipping by one by one and the thoughts of many turned towards making hay or saving turf, but a pervasive sense of gloom hung over the village of Claddaheen for Cutty the dolphin had not been seen for over a week. Everyone had heard of the accident and now the general conclusion was that the dolphin had been killed. Anna had never experienced such a sense of loss in her life — and there was dread too, dread that the graceful body of her friend might be washed ashore on some half-deserted strand. Her sleep was fitful and troubled. She often woke on those warm oppressive June nights and looked out the window on the outer reaches of the narrow cove, hoping that she would see a lissome silver body arching and diving, but she was always disappointed. Then she lay in bed staring vacantly at the ceiling and praying as she had never prayed before.

During the days she could eat very little and her mother became concerned about her and told her to take a few days off school. She had done her exams and the holidays were almost at hand. She paced about the garden, still looking down to the water that sometimes sparkled with sunlight, sometimes was clouded and grey when drifts of rain slanted in from the Atlantic. Her mother tried to distract her by giving her chores to do — cleaning a window, weeding a flower bed, herding the cows to their field — but she remained listless and lethargic. Her parents wondered if they should take Anna to the doctor but decided not to — what was happening to her was perfectly natural. She was grieving the loss of the dolphin, and it was best that she went through that grief now, no matter how painful.

There was also some disquiet in the house where Anna's uncle Tadhg lived with his wife and his step-daughter Mella. The cause was a lovable old sheepdog that had belonged to Mella's father. Mella's deep brown eyes blazed with anger when her stepfather suggested that the dog should be put down — he was old and feeble and chasing sheep across hilly ground was too much of a hardship for him.

'You never liked Rover!' Mella said resentfully as they stood in the farmyard at the back of the house. 'You were always saying he hadn't the makings of a good sheepdog — but my father knew he was the best in the world!' She tenderly stroked the old grey and white sheepdog that lay on the ground before her. She felt very protective towards him — he needed someone to defend him and since her mother was unwilling to do so, she would do it herself. Her stepfather was a tall man whose strong, finely-chiselled face always seemed stern even when he was in a good mood. He was washing one of the yard brushes in a bucket of water.

'Do you think I like seeing the dog put down?' he asked her in angry tones. 'Anyone can see that the dog is sickly. Look at his eyes, they're faded and tired, and look at how thin he is. The ribs are nearly showing through him.'

He removed the brush from the water when he had cleaned it to his satisfaction and shook it vigorously before standing it upright against the wall of an outhouse to let it dry.

'You're mean and selfish,' the girl retorted, still stroking the sheepdog.

'Tis you're the selfish one,' her stepfather countered. 'It makes no difference to me. I need a good dog and I'm getting him, but it would be an ease to that poor lad if he were dead — and if your father were alive he'd say the very same thing, mark my words.'

'But my father isn't alive is he?' the girl retorted bitterly. 'You could have saved him but you let him drown.'

Her stepfather moved towards her and took her gruffly by the arm.

'I'm sick and tired of hearing that class of talk from you, girl,' he said with determination. 'How many times do you have to be told? I did everything I could to save your father — a lot more than the two other men in the boat.'

The girl did not reply but the sullen expression on her face clearly indicated that she was less than convinced by what her stepfather had said. This was an argument they had had many times and each time her mother had intervened, urging her husband to let the matter drop. Mella had had a traumatic time of it, she said. She had been on the strand when the divers had brought her father's body ashore. She had loved her father dearly and the memory of those terrible days was bound to make her moody and irritable from time to time.

Tadhg had tried to understand, but his efforts at conciliation were often defeated by his brusque and curt manner. Now, however, he'd had enough of what he considered Mella's whinging and whimpering. She had indeed had a rough time of it but it would serve only to aggravate matters if she persisted with her delusion that he had somehow been less than wholehearted in his efforts to save her father. He held her face with his strong left hand and turned it towards him. She could think what she liked, but if he ever again heard nonsensical talk about his not trying to save her father he would not hesitate to take a strap to her.

She scowled at him defiantly, the penetrating stare of his hazel-grey eyes seeming to pierce right through her. 'And I'm taking that dog with me down to the vet's after the tea and we'll let him decide what's the right thing to be done,' he added firmly, releasing his hold on her face and making his way towards the tractor.

For those few brief moments Mella hated her stepfather as she had never hated him before. She saw Rover as one of the strongest links with her father and the good times they had shared together, and now her stepfather was trying to break that link by taking Rover from her. She felt a sudden urge to run away and to take Rover with her — an urge she had felt more than once before — but she knew in her heart of hearts that such a notion was totally impractical.

Maybe it wasn't right to be forever comparing her stepfather to her father but she couldn't help it. When her stepfather was cross with her she thought he was mean and cruel; when he tried to be nice to her she thought he was trying to wheedle his way into her emotions, trying to take her father's place which he never could. She wouldn't give him the satisfaction of taking her precious Rover down to the vet's — she would telephone the vet herself and ask him to call when he was making his rounds in the afternoon. That way she could be sure that her stepfather would not persuade him to do something he really did not want to do.

The vet did come later that afternoon, Mella waiting for him with mounting anxiety but remaining with Rover all the while. Her stepfather had not mentioned the dog at dinner — it was clear that her mother had spoken to him about it and so conversation at the table was strained and tense. The vet was an elderly man with grey hair and a beard. He was very soft-spoken and very gentle in his dealing with pets for he knew how much they meant to people. 'This old fellow's not well at all,' he told Mella openly. 'His heart-beat is very weak and he has other problems too, the poor man, so it might be kinder to do as Tadhg says.'

'But couldn't we let it go for a few days? Couldn't you give him something to try and make him better?' Mella asked in pleading tones. The old man shook his head. Rover had a good and useful life, he smiled. He had done his work well and had been a good friend to Mella and her dad, but sometimes there came a time for letting go and that time was now. Mella looked at him vaguely. Maybe what he said made sense but that still did not make the decision any easier. There was a prolonged pause as she wistfully stroked the dog again.

'Will he feel anything? Will it hurt him?' she asked at length, struggling to hold back the tears.

'It'll be just like falling asleep,' the vet assured her 'And won't you still have the memory of all the good times you've shared together.'

'If it's best for Rover ...,' she said, stroking the dog still more tenderly, and then made her way out of the yard. She did not want to be there when it happened. Mella walked slowly down the sloping boreen towards the road.

'Where are you going?' her mother called after her anxiously.

'Over to Caroline's maybe,' the girl called back.

When she went inside, the woman looked at her husband. She felt so sorry for Mella but what could she do? Should he bury the dog, Tadhg wondered, or would Mella want to do it herself?

'Better to bury him and have done with it,' the woman said. 'Better to let her remember him the way he was.'

Caroline Mason was an English artist who lived in an old-world cottage nearby. The cottage had been very run-down when she had purchased it some eight or nine years before but she had renovated it carefully, so that she did not destroy its original character. The roof had been replaced, a tiny bedroom had been converted into a kitchen, while the old kitchen — apart from being repainted — had been left intact and now served as a living room. On warm summer days Caroline put a jug of wild flowers in the hearth that was painted in a cool shade of green with its old-fashioned crane and hangers and kettles. An old chest which sometimes served as a seat was ranged along one of the rough-cast walls which were still adorned with the holy pictures and statues that had been in the cottage when the artist had bought it. She was not very religious herself, Caroline sometimes said, but she felt that the pictures and the statues were as much a part of the cottage as the stones and the mortar that had been used to build it. She had built a large room onto the back of the house and this served as her studio.

Caroline was well liked in Claddaheen. At first some of the locals thought she was mad to pay good money for a run-down old shack but they were the first to admit that she had worked wonders on the cottage and had restored it as near as anyone could to its original condition. Another attribute which endeared her to the locals was that 'she was a very handy little fiddle player.' She had studied the violin at school but had forsaken the sometimes grave and sombre classical pieces she had been required to play in those days for rousing Irish jigs and reels. She was especially liked by the children of the area who often made their way through the gateway to her cottage. She was very friendly but sometimes she placed a notice on the deep green door of the cottage telling her callers that she was at work and asking them to call back later. There was not the slightest murmur of resentment about such notices, for everyone knew how passionately Caroline devoted herself to her work. Of course when she did have callers she was more than pleased to show them her paintings in the studio and to talk to them about her work. She painted landscapes and seascapes, sometimes with figures in them. Her pictures were full of mood and atmosphere and there was a feeling of sparseness about them as if only the most essential details had been included and the rest was left to the imagination of those who viewed them.

Anna liked Caroline's paintings, particularly the strong sweeps of deep greens and browns she used to represent the fields about Claddaheen. Some people said they would prefer paintings that made things look as they really were, but Caroline would only smile and say if people wanted photographs they should go and use a camera.

That June day Caroline was sweeping the stone floor of her living room, the sunlight filtering through the tiny windows with their moss-green frames, when she saw Anna make her way across the cobbled yard. Anna wanted to tell someone outside her own family how awful she felt since Cutty had vanished from the waters about Claddaheen. The great thing about sharing a secret with Caroline was that one knew it would remain a secret. Caroline poured some lemonade and as they drank it Anna told of her sadness. The artist, who was tall and willowy with wavy black hair, was fascinated by what she heard. Did Anna really think that the dolphin had enjoyed it when she had played the tin whistle for him? She must tell her more, much more, about her emotions when she had held onto Cutty's dorsal fin and he had taken her for a ride. She herself had seen Cutty a few times and had made a few rough pencil sketches of him but she had been hoping to do a series of paintings of him — a kind of dolphin collection.

'To be honest, I didn't take much interest when I heard about him first,' Caroline admitted. 'I thought he was just another fish but then I read some of the articles about him and I discovered he wasn't a fish at all but a warm-blooded mammal, like you and me in fact.' She paused as if trying to collect her thoughts as accurately as she could. She was like that too when it came to her painting. 'I couldn't believe it when I read that the mother dolphin actually feeds her young milk,' she went on. 'Isn't that the strangest, most wonderful thing for a creature that lives in the water? And they nearly always travel in schools or groups, which made the Cladda-heen dolphin seem more fascinating still. I began to wonder why he had chosen to leave his own kind and be alone with humans.'

Anna listened intently. She could understand Caroline's enthusiasm and excitement for she had shared those feelings too.

'So I borrowed a book from the library to learn more about them,' Caroline went on. 'It says that in a group of dolphins each one has his own whistle or cry, which identifies him to the others so that they know who is calling to them.' The book was in her studio and she went to fetch it. When she returned she brought some of her own sketches also — pencil sketches which showed the dolphin humping through the waves or arching and diving or standing vertically in the water, a cheeky grin of curiosity on his face. The sketches were beautiful, Anna enthused — they really seemed to capture Cutty's mischievous and playful nature. For a little while Anna was so absorbed with the sketches and with the book that she forgot her grief.

It was not long before they were joined by Mella who told them the sad story of her father's dog. Again Caroline was full of sympathy and understanding. Anna noticed that she did not make the usual trite remarks about how Mella might feel better in a few weeks' time. If the truth were told she herself also had some reason to feel down. A bank in Dublin had been considering the possibility of buying one of her paintings for its head office. The man from the bank who had seen her work had been very enthusiastic and the sale of the painting had seemed certain, but they had changed their minds at the last moment and informed her of their decision a few hours before by telephone.

'Why don't we cheer ourselves up by going for a jaunt in my boat?' Caroline suggested. At first her guests seemed less than enthusiastic, particularly Mella. She didn't like boats and she didn't like the sea and she hated swimming. Before her father's death she had loved the sea and had often gone swimming but now no one could coax her to forsake the safety of the shore. Caroline was not discouraged however.

'Well then we'll go for a walk along the cliffs beyond the harbour. We'll drive over there and I might even do a sketch of the two of you.' This was agreed and less than twenty minutes later the girls and their companion were strolling along the cliff top. Caroline pointed to a big grey seal bottling in the water. There had been a decline in the fish catches over the past few weeks, Anna told her, and some people were blaming the seals. A few others — amongst them her Uncle Tadhg, though she did not mention him by name since Mella walked by her side — put the blame on the dolphin for this decline and they blamed him too for the nets that had been damaged, thinking that he had surged through the meshes making massive holes in them with his powerful beak.

'That couldn't be right,' Caroline answered. 'I was reading

that dolphins have a highly developed sense of echo-location which helps them to detect and avoid objects in the water.'

'What's echo-location?' Anna asked, becoming curious again.

'Well, when the dolphin makes sounds with his blowhole he is sending out a signal that bounces off objects in the water,' Caroline explained, 'and he can determine just how near or how far away any particular object is when he knows the length of time it takes the echo to return.'

'Bats do the same kind of thing, don't they?' Mella asked, plucking a rosette of sea pink that grew amongst the grasses.

'Yes they do,' the artist replied. 'So I'm sure Cutty's powers of detection would prevent him from becoming entangled in a net.'

'Most of the fishermen liked him, only a few didn't,' Anna assured her, wistfully looking out to sea all the while, hoping to catch a glimpse of her wonderful friend, but there was only the island and the birds and the seals.

Soon Caroline asked the two girls to sit on the grass. Mella was still holding the rosette of sea pink on its smoothly rounded stem. Her stepfather would have probably buried poor Rover by now, she mused, idly plucking the petals of the densely packed flowers and scattering them like confetti in the wind.

Caroline took out her sketch pad and began to make a pencil sketch of the girls: fair Anna in a yellow dress, freckle-face Mella in a tee-shirt and jeans. It was amazing how one wild creature, the dolphin, had made such an impact on the lives of so many people, for apart from a few misguided fishermen he had won the hearts of all who had seen him. She herself had even ordered a wet suit from Dublin with the intention of getting close to him, but all her plans had come to nothing and she was really disappointed that she would not be able to proceed with her dolphin paintings. Slowly the sketch developed on the page. The girls talked about many things — school and basketball and music and television programmes — but soon they became restless again and all three of them continued with their walk.

Some time later they were driving back through the village when Anna's father waved at Caroline to slow down and came running towards them. There had just been a report on Radio Kerry that a dolphin had been found stranded on a beach between Milltown and Killorglin, he told them, and they could hear the excitement in his voice. A place called Callin, he went on, and some fishermen there had somehow managed to return the dolphin to the tide. Anna's heart began to drum again. Could it have been Cutty? Her father suggested they drive to Callin to make further enquiries. It was twenty miles away but the fishermen would surely have noticed if the dolphin had a bad gash on his back or on his side. Who knew, maybe someone had taken some photographs, though the radio report had made no mention of any. Anna beamed with joy. It was decided that they would all go home first and have a quick bite to eat. Caroline had done enough driving for one day, Anna's father insisted, and so they would travel in his car. An hour later they were on the road, heading towards Milltown. Anna's eyes began to sparkle again.

CHAPTER FIVE

There was animated conversation as they drove along and the talk was of nothing but dolphins. Anna's father told how he had read in one of the articles about Cutty that the presence of a dolphin helped people who were depressed or nervous. Caroline said that the same point had been made in the book she had read and she would be inclined to believe it. After all, every fibre of Cutty's being seemed to be imbued with a sense of fun and joy and he had an amazing ability to communicate that zest for life to others.

Mella listened intently but said nothing; if only Caroline had heard her stepfather say he was glad to see the back of the dolphin for they hadn't had a decent catch since he had made his first appearance in the waters off Claddaheen. Tadhg knew all the old superstitions and believed most of them. If a farmer interfered with a swallow's nest his cows would milk blood; if the cock crowed at night then something untoward was sure to happen; when a cat licked and washed himself, bad luck would fall on the first person he fixed his gaze upon the moment he had finished his task.

There were others who remembered these old beliefs too but they did not take them as seriously as Tadhg who was sometimes manipulated by the wily Eamonn King. His attitude towards the seals was somewhat mixed; he had this strange notion that they were people under some kind of enchantment and he had scores of stories about mother seals suckling human babies at their breasts, seals giving fishermen rides on their backs, seals keening at the death of one of their number. But he hated them too for they ate great quantities of herring and salmon. Tadhg was one of those people who was reassured by all that was customary and familiar; he disliked innovations and mistrusted strangers. That in essence was why he was glad the dolphin was no longer seen at Claddaheen.

'I don't think it's right that dolphins should be captured and made do tricks for people,' Anna said earnestly. It was a sentiment she had expressed many many times in her dolphin diary. 'Dolphins are meant to be wild and free and they're not supposed to act like monkeys in a circus.'

'Maybe it isn't all bad,' Caroline replied as the car passed through the village of Castlemaine and a man in a doorway gave them a friendly wave. 'Maybe captured dolphins help people to appreciate how wonderful dolphins are — and how many people get the chance to see a dolphin in the wild?'

'But the most important thing to a dolphin is his freedom; it's because they're free that they jump for joy,' Anna said. 'They only jump in tanks and things when they want to be rewarded with a fish.'

As they chatted the time passed quickly and it wasn't long before Anna and her father, Caroline and Mella found themselves on the strand at Callin. Two boats at anchor on the tide rocked gently in the breeze. A cormorant was standing on a rock, its great black wings outstretched. A fisherman was tarring an upturned boat a little distance along the strand and the newcomers walked towards him. Anna's father introduced himself and the others to the fisherman and explained their interest in the dolphin.

'The dolphin, is it?' the man at the boat said smiling. He was going slightly bald on top and there was a twinkle in his eyes. 'He caused more excitement than the visit of the Pope. 'Twas myself spotted him when I was working in the field beyond,' he went on. 'I didn't know what to make of him; first I thought he was a dead calf or a sheep for 'twould amaze you what some people fling into the rivers.' He abandoned his tarring for a few minutes; he would show them exactly where the dolphin had been stranded. 'Well, when I came down and saw what was before me I got an awful fright and the first thing I did was to run up for buckets and douse him with water for the poor lad's skin looked very dry. The tide was far out but I kept at it, in and out with the buckets till he was well soaked.'

'But how did you manage to get him back into the water?' Anna's father asked, looking at the tracks of large tractor wheels still visible in the mud. 'Well, I says to Mag, the Missus, to telephone Frankeen, the vet,' the fisherman went on, delighted with the newcomers' interest, 'for it wasn't long before some of the lads came on the scene and we might do more damage than good when we didn't know what we should do!'

'And what did the vet say?' Anna asked, fixing her gaze on the undulating green of the tide, where clumps of bladderwrack were drifting here and there.

'Frankeen advised us to keep the water to the dolphin,' the storyteller explained, 'and we were getting right worried when in the heel of the hunt he lands with this kind of a sling that looked for all the world like a stretcher and it lined with rubbery foam.' He paused as if seeing the moment clearly in his mind's eye and remembering it with great relish, since he himself had been one of the leading players. 'Frankeen supervised operations as we pushed the dolphin onto the sling, making great laws, warning us to be specially careful with the flippers for they were very delicate, he said; there was great commotion, whatever the poor dolphin made of it all, for however they got wind of it half the children of the parish were swarming round us and they running helter-skelter with buckets of water.' He paused again and looked at his listeners with serious intent. 'It would have been a crying shame if the poor lad had died for he was a gallant soldier and didn't make a bit of fuss.'

Anna longed to ask the vital question about the gash but if their informant had seen it he would surely mention it in due course ... and if she did ask the question and the answer was negative she would have no great enthusiasm to hear the remainder of the story. 'Well, however we managed it with all the *ruaille buaille*, we got the dolphin onto the sling and then we hitched the sling onto Frankeen's landrover and he drove out to the water. We thought all was grand but we had to run out and do more manoeuvring to get the dolphin out of the sling and into the tide.' They turned and walked back towards the upturned boat again, while the man went on with his story. 'You could see the life coming back into him when the water started to roll over him again as soon as we tipped him into it, and very slow tipping it was. There was great cheering and clapping when he started to swim — 'twas better than a win in the lottery.' A broad smile radiated across the fisherman's face. That was a moment he would never forget.

'The biggest problem apart from his skin would be his

breathing,' Caroline explained. 'Dolphins are weightless in the water but when they become stranded the pressure of gravity and the weight of their bodies makes it very difficult for them to fill and empty their lungs.'

The vet had been telling them things like that afterwards, the fisherman added, for they had gone for a celebration in the pub — and why shouldn't they celebrate, for wasn't the dolphin back where he belonged? Anna liked the blue-eyed fisherman; he wasn't boasting: he was just eager to tell them what a wonderful experience the saving of the dolphin had been. Then he said something which made her heart drum with excitement. 'The lads were saying he must have had a few scrapes before, for there was a big wound in his left side like he might be after banging it against a rock or something.'

'Was it getting better or did it look infected?' Caroline asked, translating Anna's thoughts into words.

'Frankeen had a good look at it and he said 'twas coming on grand and then he gave us a bit of a lecture about the healing power of nature, he's a bit like that at times.'

There followed a hearty laugh, but Anna could scarcely contain her wild delight. Cutty was alive and well — and there was every chance that if his confidence in humankind had been shattered by the accident with the boats it had now been well and truly restored by the kindness of his rescuers. 'Has he been seen since?' she asked, the tremor in her voice betraying her emotion.

The dolphin had given a few sweeps about the mouth of the cove, the fisherman told her, and had then headed out to sea. Though he was thankful to his rescuers, it was as if he wanted to get far away from the shore.

Anna's expression was full of intensity again. Was it possible that Cutty held the same feeling towards the waters of Claddaheen or would the bond he had formed with her be strong enough to overcome any fears he might have? This latter thought filled her with renewed hope and nothing could diminish the sensation of relief and joy. Cutty was alive and that was all that mattered. She would not so readily give up the hope that he might return to Claddaheen one day soon.

Next day Donal and Tom were diving in the grey-green waters to the east of Puffin Island where they had located the rotting timbers of the *San Juan*. It was with considerable difficulty that Donal had kept his secret, especially since he had again been taunted by Eamonn in the pub. The two friends were persevering with their task and were investigating in minute detail the area of seabed where the boards were strewn. They were gradually coming to the conclusion that they would have to extend the range of their dive, for the shifts in the currents off the island were so strong, especially in winter time, that any artefacts from the ship which still survived could have been carried a long way from their original resting place when the ship went down. Or maybe it was the other way round, maybe it was the planks and the mast pole that had been shifted in the current; probably the heavy metal objects such as the siege guns and the cannon remained in the same positions they had found hundreds of years before. Yes, that was surely it, Donal told his friend when they returned to the boat for a rest. They would have to dive in a new area of water some distance away. If they came upon the cannon they would surely have discovered the precise location where the *San Juan* had come to grief. And where they found the cannon there too they might find one of the metal trunks full of coins that were reputedly on board the Armada ships. That was a prospect that filled Donal with renewed excitement. Despite all that claptrap about the best things in life being free, money was power, he insisted, the brine dripping from his wet suit as he held a mug of coffee in one hand and a cigarette in the other. The coffee flask was in a basket on the floor of the boat.

When he had finished the coffee, he rested his back across the timber seats of the boat and peered up at the sky, his legs sprawled wide apart. 'The best way to impress a girl is with money,' he mused, and Tom laughed. Donal took occasional drags of the cigarette between his lips, slow deliberate drags, making delicious rings of smoke with his mouth. If they found the gold he wouldn't mind a big mansion with a swimming pool and a jacuzzi and maybe an island of his own and a plane and a yacht.

Tom, who was sitting on the stern of the boat, smiled again, his curly black hair dripping wet. 'It might be better to find the gold first,' he suggested, 'and to make plans afterwards.'

'The trouble with you, Tom, is you've no faith and no imagination,' Donal told him seriously. 'I know you say you're interested in the historical significance of the thing and you're delighted with what we've found already and you don't really care if we find anything more, but if you tell the truth you're just as anxious to find the gold as I am.'

'We might get some kind of reward,' Tom mused. 'I could get rid of that banger of a car I have, for one thing, and get a souped-up little number like yours.'

'Is that all? Don't go too wild, will you?' Donal retorted in his good-humoured way. 'I want some of the good life and I mean to get it.'

'Look around you,' Tom suggested with a sweep of his hand, 'Maybe you have the good life already and you don't know it.'

'Ah, don't give me that crap. I get enough of that at home,' the other replied more grimly. 'The old man never stops going on at me but he doesn't have to look too far to see where

I get my liking for money.' He paused and shielded his eyes with his hands. 'On second thoughts, people like you are better off being poor, Tom; you don't appreciate the beauty of money.'

Sometimes Tom could not decide when Donal was in earnest or when he was in a mocking mood but the one good thing about him was that life was never boring when he was around.

Some time later the two friends sped to a different location and dived again, bubbles gurgling to the surface as they sank into the sunlit waters that were more translucent than they had been in recent days. At first their search seemed hopeless but then Tom's gaze was attracted towards a rusty metal cylinder on the floor of the sea. He reached out and rubbed the surface of the metal, encrusted here and there with barnacles and limpets. This must be one of the elusive cannons from the *San Juan*! He looked around, preparing to signal to Donal, but Donal had swum elsewhere and there was no trace of him. Part of the heavy metal tube was embedded in the sea bed but what was visible clearly indicated that it could not have served any function other than that of a cannon. He held his flashlight close to the opening and shone it into the tube. It was such a strange sensation, for he was surely the first person who had come close to the cannon since it had been put on board the *San Juan*, when it sailed from Lisbon on May 30, 1588 under the command of the Duke of Medina Sidonia. Strange, so strange, to think that so many proud ships had met their doom off the Irish coast. Tom swam about the cannon for a little while and soon he made another discovery: a plate made of some kind of metal. He deposited it in the transparent plastic bag he had brought with him.

Suddenly a great grey mass went zooming by him. He remained motionless in the water; it couldn't be the dolphin, or could it? Seconds later his speculations were proved to be correct when the dolphin hung in the water directly before him and eyed him intently. A glow of warmth seemed to radiate through Tom's body when he saw those smiling lips, those expressive eyes. Cutty had surely heard the clatter of the plate when he had lifted it from the sea bed. But then the dolphin began to twist and turn, darting and diving this way and that as if he were distressed about something. Tom observed his actions intently. Another time it might have seemed to him that the dolphin merely wanted him to join in his frolics in the water, but now his movements communicated an unmistakable sense of urgency. Sometimes when he darted away he tilted his head sideways as if he wanted the diver to follow him. At first Tom was unsure but then he made up his mind and swam after the dolphin. Whatever Donal might say Tom was elated to find that he had survived the accident and returned to his old familiar territory. But where was Donal? Just then he saw the shadow of his friend struggling in the greeny distance. He swam furiously towards him, the friendly dolphin darting away or diving low only to reappear seconds later.

'Bad cramps,' Donal gasped through his mouthpiece. His right leg was rigid and cold, the flipper on his left leg flicking frantically backwards and forwards. Then the dolphin did the strangest thing of all; he swam under the stricken diver's chest and attempted to prop him up with his hump. Donal could scarcely believe what was happening. The dolphin remained in that position for only a few vital seconds until Tom came to Donal's aid, but for Donal they were the most unbelievable moments of his life. He had heard some of the villagers claim that dolphins came to the aid of drowning swimmers but he had scoffed at their naive delusions as he would scoff at people who believed in banshees. Now, as the dolphin came beneath him, the fearful drumming of his heart began to slacken and his sense of relief was such that he could physically feel the vibrations of fear draining from his body. Then before he knew it Tom was grabbing him by the arm and lifting him slowly to the surface. The dolphin slipped effortlessly away the moment he sensed the danger had passed. If the divers rose too quickly, however, they knew they would succumb to the dreaded 'bends' because of the great pressure underwater, so their progress upwards was slow and deliberate.

When Tom had finally lifted his companion into the boat he looked about to see if he could catch a glimpse of the handsome dolphin. Donal struggled to remove his face mask, gasping all the while. He had never been so terrified in his life, he admitted, forgetting his usual bravado; for a few seconds there he was sure he was a goner and then as if to add to his terror the stupid dolphin had brushed past him once or twice before vanishing again. Now he was certain that the dolphin had swum about him a few times to satisfy himself that he really was in trouble and was not playing some silly game. 'Imagine being saved by a dolphin!'

'And you were the one who said he was a nuisance and wished he would take himself elsewhere,' Tom replied still casting his eyes about for a glimpse of the hero.

'Don't rub it in, Tom,' his companion retorted with a shiver. He felt suddenly cold. When Tom had pulled himself aboard they prepared to return to the shore.

Seconds later Cutty launched himself into an explosive leap, slicing the air with the arch of his body and sending swirls of spray shooting through the air. 'Thanks pal. Thanks with all my heart!' Donal called out to him. More spectacular leaping and diving followed — the dolphin's dance of cele-bration, as if he knew that he had done a kindly deed.

CHAPTER SIX

In a matter of days Cutty was a hero and Donal was a celebrity as he told everyone he met how the dolphin had come to his aid. As his diving partner had anticipated, he was tempted at last to show off the plate and the medal they had found on the ocean floor.

'You've really gone and blown it now,' Tom assured him but he was not really annoyed about it. Of course he would have preferred if their finds had remained a secret for a little while longer but there was some satisfaction in the knowledge that if any further significant finds were made they would know that the grave of the *San Juan* had first been discovered by himself and Donal. As soon as Donal had displayed the medal and the plate to all and sundry Tom had taken the precaution of telephoning the County Council offices in Tralee in the hope that they might arrange to send out some more expert divers to explore the site professionally. But it was the dolphin's act of kindness which fired the imagination of the people of Claddaheen, and though they knew that Donal was prone to exaggeration, they were sure that the incident had taken place just as he had described it because the more reliable Tom verified every word.

There have been times in history when whole populations have succumbed to gold fever but now those who lived in the village and the townland of Claddaheen gladly submerged themselves in dolphin fever. Boatloads of locals and tourists alike were ferried out to see the dolphin at the mouth of the harbour. There were shrieks of delight when Cutty made one of his spectacular leaps or when he rode the bow waves of the boats. The name that Anna had given to him was now on everyone's lips though most people did not know or did not care where the name had originated. It was a very good name for him, people said, for as soon as his dorsal fin appeared in the distance he could be seen cutting through the water with effortless grace. Very rarely did he disappoint the passengers, for he was almost always in a boisterous playful mood, and he seemed to regard the happy shrieks as a kind of applause for his displays. This was the first time that the vast majority of those in the boats had ever seen a wild dolphin, and the memory of that first encounter would remain with them forever. The trips became so popular that soon extra boats were laid on to deal with the crowds. Waves of cameramen seemed to descend upon the place as news of Cutty's kindly deed began to circulate more widely. 'It's come to the stage,' said an old woman wryly, 'where you'd be half afraid to open the newspaper for fear you'd see Donal Jones' mug grinning out at you.'

There was talk of the dolphin in the streets, in the shops and in the pubs. Donal's father commissioned a new sign in the shape of a dolphin and hastily rechristened his guest house The Dolphin Inn. He was not the only one to get that idea for in a matter of days the village boasted two Dolphin

Pubs, a Dolphin Craft Shop and a Dolphin Grocery Shop — all having abandoned their former trade names. The arty-crafty lady in the craftshop wore garish dolphin earrings and encouraged her customers to do likewise — or perhaps they might prefer a dolphin brooch or a dolphin bracelet? The local photographer had published a series of dolphin postcards and they were selling, he said, as fast as people could lick the stamps on them, heading for destinations all over Europe.

Cutty even got a mention in the church and it was a mention which made Anna very happy. There was nothing wrong in exploiting the dolphin to develop trade, Father McCarthy said; they were only doing what people every-where would do if they were blessed with such a welcome guest. Yes, the dolphin was a blessing but they must never forget that he was a living creature, a mysterious creature of the deep with needs of his own and like most other living creatures he needed to be on his own from time to time; he needed time to rest and relax.

Anna smiled when she heard these words. It was now almost the end of July and Anna's dolphin diary bulged with entries of every kind, mainly accounts of her own experiences with Cutty but with passing references to the experiences of others too. She had been overjoyed when she had first heard of Cutty's return to Claddaheen and impressed when she had heard of how gallantly he had come to Donal's rescue but her pleasure had been tinged with strange feelings of resentment and envy. She had come to regard Cutty as very much her own dolphin, but now there was a special bond between him and Donal too. Though she raced down to the strand the moment she heard of his return, for a day or two it seemed as if Cutty would never come back to their secret place. She had told Caroline Mason of her secret encounters with the dolphin and Caroline suggested that she might come down to the cove and wait with Anna there. At first the notion of sharing Cutty with yet another person did not appeal to Anna, but Caroline was different — she was a sensitive person and understood how Anna felt about the dolphin.

'I've got a little inflatable boat and we can row it out with paddles,' said Caroline.

This was agreed and this was what they did. Just when it seemed that Cutty had quite forgotten his friendship with Anna he came cruising through the water late one evening when the sun was a gigantic fireball in the west and the waters were streaked with burnished gold. Anna's eyes sparkled with joy; it was like a scene from a fairytale to see the dolphin zooming through the gently undulating waters that were blue-black and golden. Caroline thought it was brilliant too — it was like having a private audience with some famous star. At first Cutty made wide arches and circles about the inflatable boat; he had never encountered a boat of any kind in these waters before and so his movements seemed to reveal some uncertainty. It was as if he had expected to be greeted by the familiar sight of Anna swimming in the water and now here was something unexpected. After some moments of circling, Anna watching him with wild delight all the while, he dived beneath the surface and vanished without trace. 'I wonder if he's gone again,' Caroline whispered, her eyes shining too. The timidity of that whisper suggested that she was afraid that any words of hers might break the spell of these enchanted moments. She had been many places, seen many sights but nothing surpassed the beauty of the dolphin in the darkened waters that were finely streaked with gold.

Then suddenly Cutty began to prod the bottom of the inflatable with his powerful beak, causing it to bob up and down. This was done so playfully that Anna and Caroline were not afraid. Indeed Caroline had heard some of the divers say that Cutty often behaved in this way — and perhaps in this instance there was some purpose to his prodding and bumping for he was surely investigating the inflatable with his keen sense of touch. Caroline reached down and took her violin in her hands, urging Anna to take her tin whistle too. Soon the evening stillness was filled with the jaunty rhythmic lilt of 'The Kerry Dances'. Cutty began to hump and dive about the boat again as the two friends played to their hearts' content; seconds later a cheeky head popped through the water and two beautiful little eyes sparkled with interest. Then the head shook from side to side and Cutty began to chatter as Anna had never heard him chatter before. Caroline broke into song in a moment of spontaneous joy: *'Oh the days of the Kerry dances, oh the ring of the piper's tune, oh for one of those hours of gladness, gone alas like our youth too soon.'*

Anna placed her tin whistle aside for a moment and reached out her hand, touching the side of Cutty's head. 'Welcome home, Cutty, welcome home,' she said with a warmth that the dolphin could not fail to appreciate. Next moment he darted a little distance away, full of high spirits and animation, and flung himself high into the air, his body invigorated by the splash of golden spray and the magic of the music. More boisterous leaping and diving followed. The two friends were celebrating his return with music and song and he was sharing in their sense of revelry in his own riotous way. After a pause they played another tune for Cutty and this time they chose the haunting beautiful strains of 'The Cúileann'. Caroline was an excellent musician and though her companion's music was less than perfect it did not seem to matter a whit, for there they were — a woman, a girl and a dolphin — in a world all of their own, a golden sunset world of music and sea. And Cutty seemed to appreciate the change of mood for whereas 'The Kerry Dances' had encouraged explosive leaping and diving, 'The Cúileann' evoked a gentler response as he humped merrily, playfully up and down.

That Sunday late in July when Father McCarthy mentioned the dolphin in his sermon, Anna smiled, remembering the day the dolphin had danced to their music. That had almost been a fortnight before, and what fun they'd had in the interval. Caroline had never worn a wet suit before and it was so funny to watch her try it on for the first time. She would be worn out by the time she got into the water she said, and Anna grinned. Caroline was behaving like a little girl, a fact which had not escaped Caroline herself, but she did not care for she had never been so excited in her life. Then one evening the two of them jumped into the water, Anna with her snorkel on her head. Cutty came to investigate the newcomer, butting her gently with his beak or bumping her back from behind. He liked Caroline immediately for she made no sudden moves to grab at his dorsal fin as a few divers had done in the harbour. When they had done this he had clearly resented it and had zoomed suddenly away. That was why Anna felt very special indeed; he had allowed her to hold fast to his dorsal fin and had given her a fantastic ride, but now that he had returned would he allow her to do so again? Some of the divers whose advances Cutty had promptly rejected claimed he seemed hostile and aggressive when he had shaken them off.

Much had happened since Anna had taken her first whimsical ride. Cutty had been badly injured by the speedboat; the gash in his side had healed but was still clearly visible; he had withdrawn from human contact for some time and even though he seemed as friendly as ever since his return would he allow her to come as close as before? That was the question which nagged at Anna now and then as she swam with Caroline and Cutty in the water. And would Caroline's presence make a difference? A dolphin could kill a whale or a shark by butting it with his beak and there was devastating power in his massive flukes. Though she did not know Cutty's precise weight she could guess from what she had read that he must be at least six hundred pounds. One blow of the tail and she would be sent spinning to the depths. Yet she felt a compelling urge to share another magical ride with the fabulous Cutty. He was now clearly intrigued by Caroline, rolling and curling and curving about her, gently nudging and bumping her from time to time. Any feelings Anna had of wanting to keep Cutty all to herself had now disappeared and it made her truly happy to see Caroline so excited and elated at her first meeting with the dolphin in his own element.

Anna marvelled again at Cutty's mastery in the bracingly cold water — his artful dipping and diving, his graceful cutting and cruising, his explosive launching and leaping. His body could not have been more perfectly streamlined for a life in the ocean. She marvelled too at his amazing capacity to change not only his posture but also his pace in a matter of seconds. Then Caroline decided on a game of hide and seek, moving away and remaining perfectly still near the far side of the inflatable. Cutty seemed baffled as he looked about for her but then he dived suddenly and it was only a matter of moments before he was nudging her from behind, catching her unawares.

When Caroline clambered on board the boat, Anna and Cutty remained in the water together. Now they were both in a gentle mood, the dolphin brushing close to the girl's body as if to show her that he was eager to renew their special friendship. And then Anna summoned her courage once more and took hold of his powerful dorsal fin. Seconds later the dream had begun again and she was riding the waves with the grace and speed of the dolphin beside her. Caroline sat in the boat and gasped in amazement. The dolphin was cutting through the sun-splashed waters, the great red fireball that was the sun itself sinking still deeper and deeper in western skies, the girl being swept along at such incredible speed that she left a trail of spume in her wake. The artist reached for her camera. This would make a dramatic photograph and at some future time she might need convincing that it had actually happened and had not been a dream. The camera clicked once, then twice then three times but neither the dolphin nor his companion seemed aware of it. Again Anna felt as if she could empathise with the creatures of the sea that spend all their lives in the water. She wished the ride would go on forever, but inevitably it ended, Cutty gradually slowing his pace before hanging motionless in the water. Anna coughed and gasped for air before blowing him a kiss of thanks.

Caroline said she could stay forever with the dolphin in the water, but if she did she would never get any work done. So from that time onwards each time Cutty visited the cove, Anna frolicked with him as before but Caroline busied herself with her sketching and painting. Sometimes she sat in the inflatable, her sketch pad on her knees; sometimes she took as her vantage point a nearby formation of rocks; sometimes she set up her easel on the strand. She always chose the same subject, the girl and the dolphin, trying to interpret and portray the wonderful relationship between them in all its varying moods and tones. Caroline was so passionate about her work that she hated being disturbed, which was why the little sheltered cove was so perfect, for while part of it was visible from the farmhouse high on the hillside, it was almost completely hidden from the view of those who travelled the road above it. The artist spent a great deal of time over each painting, putting the finishing touches to it at home in her studio in the cottage. If she maintained the same level of concentration she would soon have enough for a collection.

~

Anna waited at the church gates for her mother who was chatting with a neighbour. She saw Donal and Tom talking to some of the lads and Donal was telling them of the games he played with Cutty. Boatloads of divers had been swarming over the grave of the *San Juan* for the past while, but though they had found interesting objects such as bowls and tankards not one of them had yet found a single Spanish coin. Cutty was always diving with him these days, Donal said, for now he and the dolphin were the best of friends and sometimes he heard the dolphin making clicking noises of delight. Donal's listeners were intrigued by his tales for dolphin mania was still as potent as ever in Claddaheen. If there was any doubt of that one had only to take note of the diversity of accents in the church yard and on the streets — strangers everywhere and all of them lured by the spell of the dolphin. 'He loves it when I toss him a fish from the boat,' Donal went on with a grin. 'Myself and Tom, we see the silver fish shooting through the air for a split second but it hardly ever has time to land on the surface for Cutty always jumps high — like Jack O'Shea in a Munster final — and before you know it the poor fish is gone.'

'And the best of it all,' Tom intervened with the same enthusiasm, 'is that Cutty brought us a fish in return once or twice.'

'Ah, he's a good lad,' Donal went on, warming to his subject. 'Bringing us the fish is his way of showing how much he likes to share.'

Anna grinned — if they only knew of the fabulous experiences she and Caroline had had with the dolphin.

Mella's stepfather Tadhg, however, had never welcomed Cutty's presence. Most of those who heard his objections concluded that he was just being superstitious — he feared the dolphin in the same way that he feared a lone magpie or a rabbit or a red-haired woman — but Tadhg had another reason for disliking the dolphin, one which had not eluded his wife and stepdaughter. Tadhg sometimes went poaching for salmon, setting his nets and leaving them in place during the course of the night, which was against the law. Tadhg's poaching partner was the sullen and peevish Eamonn who was always getting into arguments about politics or religion in the pub. Eamonn had a flabby rotund face with round brown eyes and thinning blonde hair, his chin also covered with a thin and fuzzy growth of hair. It was amazing that Eamonn and Tadhg got on reasonably well together for they were both quarrelsome at the best of times, the sly Eamonn sometimes fanning the flames of his companion's superstitions about the dolphin.

Early on Monday morning a boat moved silently out into the still grey tide, both men rowing hard. They used monofilament nets which were very difficult to see and which were also against the law. Cutty could easily detect the presence of the nets, however, by bouncing sound signals off them but when some helpless salmon became entangled in the meshes he often came to investigate the cause of the vibrations. Now he was swimming round a trapped salmon. As the fishing boat drew near, he suddenly became aware of the rhythmic rise and fall of the oars and zoomed away, avoiding the nets with uncanny ease. The men in the boat caught a glimpse of his dorsal fin slicing through the water.

'The fat cats in this town getting rich on the back of that

stupid dolphin,' Eamonn said bitterly. 'Dolphin brooches, dolphin jumpers, dolphin postcards — anything for a quick buck.'

'Aye, and they'd persuade you black and blue that he doesn't get near enough to a net to damage it,' Mella's step-father agreed. There was scorn and disgust in his tone. 'Tis the seals damage the nets, they say, and still they can't give me one good reason why it's been the worst fishing season in history when anyone with two eyes can see the reason is that dolphin.' He released his grip on the oars and began to struggle with the net. 'He must eat all 'round him and he must frighten off as much again.'

'What do they care about you and your fish as long as they're lining their own pockets?' Eamonn scoffed. 'Donal the fancy boy with his sports car and his speedboat making business for his father with some cock and bull story about the dolphin saving his life.'

He reached down, pushed a plank aside and produced a cloth scabbard. Next moment he withdrew a huge knife, with a long shimmering blade that tapered to a point at the tip. He skimmed a finger gently down the edge of the blade, his dark eyes shining with malice. 'Killed a shark with this one time,' he boasted, 'and the water was red with blood.' He paused, glanced at his companion and eyed the blade again with a malevolent grin. 'Wouldn't it be a real shame if the dolphin were to end his days with this little beauty stuck through his belly?' Seconds later he had returned the knife to its scabbard and was helping his accomplice with the task of hauling in the net.

CHAPTER SEVEN

On the first Tuesday in August Anna sat in the old-fashioned living room of Caroline's cottage and listened intently as the artist told her what she had heard in the village. She had been down to the craft shop making arrangements to have some of her dolphin paintings framed and Dolly who owned the craft shop had had some exciting news for her. If the truth were known, Dolly generally had exciting news about anything and everything of local interest, not always accurate. She looked ridiculous in her oversized dolphin earrings, while her ankle-length cotton dress was a throw-back to the sixties, but then she liked being different because it made people notice her and talk about her. She had heard that an independent film production company was coming to Claddaheen in the near future; they hadn't decided yet if there would be enough material to make an entire programme about Cutty or whether they would slot the sequences they filmed at Claddaheen into a general documentary about the sea. They should be able to get some exciting footage: Cutty in full flight when he launched himself high into the air or riding the bow waves of the boats when he escorted them in and out of the harbour or accompanying the divers when they explored the scattered remnants of the *San Juan*, but would it be enough to fill an entire programme?

'They'll surely want to talk to you about your paintings and to include some of them in the film,' Anna enthused. 'And when they ask me about the girl in the water with him?' Caroline prompted. 'Tell them there was no girl — that she was just imaginary — we agreed about that, didn't we?' Anna replied with some apprehension.

'Yes we did,' her companion agreed, 'but that was before we heard about the film crew coming to Claddaheen. A few shots of you with Cutty would be the most spectacular of all, and they'd give a lot of pleasure to a great many people.'

'But then we couldn't have our secret times with him any more,' Anna countered with a frown which indicated that the notion of becoming part of the film did not appeal to her in the slightest. 'Our secret cove would be invaded and Cutty would miss his games with us.'

Caroline rubbed her hand through her short black hair and thought awhile. The dolphin really did seem to enjoy their company; he had come to regard the cove as a place of refuge, a sanctuary where he could maintain contact with human-kind but where he could also relax and do entirely as he pleased. Yet he had given them so much happiness and his relationship with Anna was so beautiful it seemed a shame not to share that beauty. Cutty's cheeky chattering and lively acrobatics would make excellent viewing but if a few sequences of the girl and the dolphin were featured they would add another dimension to the film entirely.

Anna however remained unconvinced. 'He's not a circus animal and I'm not going to make him act like one,' she insisted. 'After all, the people round here have done well enough out of him and if we become too greedy we might frighten him away for good.'

'It's your decision and I won't press you to change your mind,' Caroline answered, 'but never in a million years could a wild dolphin like Cutty be regarded as a circus animal.' She rose and made her way to the adjoining studio where Anna again admired some of the dolphin paintings, all of them still carefully stored in a large leather folder.

'Do you really think a circus animal would inspire me in this way?' Caroline went on.

'They're beautiful,' Anna said with genuine enthusiasm.

'Thank you,' Caroline answered, 'but if I hadn't had the privilege of seeing you and Cutty in the water together the paintings would not nearly be as exciting as they are. I think it's going to be the same with the film.' Anna agreed to think about it but she still believed that Cutty was far more important than any film and anything which posed the slightest threat to his welfare was to be shunned at all costs.

As she walked home Anna was thinking of Mella who longed to swim in the sea with Cutty but was terrified of getting into the water. Even boats frightened her. Sometimes Anna saw her ambling idly amongst the lobster pots on the pier and wistfully looking out towards the mouth of the harbour. The sadness in her eyes was unmistakable when she heard the squeals of joy of those on board the boats as Cutty made another spectacular leap into the air. Once or twice when Anna and her father had gone out to set lobster pots, Anna had tried to cajole her into coming with them, but Mella always had some excuse: her mother was expecting her home to paint the garden gate or her stepfather would be cross with her if she were late for supper. Yet Anna remained convinced that as soon as Mella became engrossed with Cutty's antics it would not be long before she forgot the terror of the sea that had haunted her ever since that stormy night when her father had lost his life. Caroline's inflatable was still moored down at the cove and when Anna had consulted her father on the matter she telephoned Mella and asked her to meet her at the cove that evening.

Mella was a little intrigued by Anna's call but evening time found her on the strand at the cove at the appointed time. 'Will you come for a row in the inflatable?' Anna asked with a twinkle in her eyes. 'The water's very calm and shallow here.'

'You know I don't like boats,' Mella answered, a shiver tingling down her spine.

'I know you don't like boats but if we go out just a little bit we may see the dolphin — he comes here almost every day,' Anna encouraged.

'I've seen the dolphin,' her friend replied fidgeting with a shell in her hands.

'Yes but only at a distance. He's fabulous when you see him really close up,' Anna went on with the same enthusiasm as before.

'And why did you ask me to bring my flute?' Mella wondered.

'Cutty loves music. He leaps and splashes and dives when I play the tin whistle for him.' Anna smiled. 'It'd be great if you played a tune on the flute for him too.' She paused and stepped into the inflatable. 'Ah, come on, Mella,' she pleaded, 'we'll only go out a small bit.' Mella hesitated a moment, retrieved her flute from a rock where she had put it for safe keeping and took a tentative step on board the boat. She shivered and felt cold again. Her fear of the water went very deep; she had seen the men drag her father's lifeless body ashore and it was an image which would always remain with her. Anna took the paddles in her hands, reassuring her companion again that they would travel only a little distance from the shore. Mella looked about; the water was blue and glassy and yet she could not feel at ease. Anna was making gallant efforts to distract her with stories of the wonderful experiences she herself had shared with the dolphin. She glanced at her watch; it was about time for Cutty to make his usual appearance. She urged Mella to play a tune on the flute. Mella grasped the instrument with trembling fingers and began to play. Anna looked anxiously about, hoping against hope that Cutty would not let her down this evening of all evenings when his coming might make such a difference to Mella's life.

There were a few moments of suspense, but then the graceful Cutty came humping towards them and Mella felt a sudden surge of elation sweep through her body. She felt an overwhelming sense of relief too for whenever her friends had shared their stories of Cutty she had no story to tell, no proud moment of contact with the friendly wild dolphin to describe, but now all that was about to change.

Cutty curled about the inflatable for quite some time, his body radiating exuberance and energy and a wild kind of zest that could scarcely be described. Still Mella played on the flute and Anna could see the old familiar light begin to flicker in her eyes. When the music stopped Cutty came close to the inflatable, hung in a vertical position and popped his head through the water.

'Reach out and touch him,' Anna encouraged.

Mella moved her fingers cautiously, tentatively towards the dolphin's head; his beautiful eyes seemed to be looking straight at her and he seemed to sense her timidity for he remained almost perfectly motionless. When her fingers came into contact with the skin she gave a gasp of admiration and incredulity; it was a sensation that filled her with a depth of happiness she had not known for weeks and months and years.

Anna could scarcely remember when she had seen Cutty so gentle and so timid but then his response to Mella did not surprise her in the least, for he was a warm-hearted intelligent fellow. The rapport he had developed with humankind was amazing — and even more so was his ability to distinguish individuals' needs and desires. The smile that beamed from Mella's face spoke more truths than a thousand books. She began to talk to the wild dolphin as if he had been a lifelong friend. She might have felt foolish talking to a stray dog or cat but she thought it the most natural thing in the world to talk to the dolphin, and for a few moments she seemed scarcely aware that Anna was beside her in the boat.

'He's more beautiful than they say,' she said turning to her companion at last and the dolphin began to indulge in graceful rolling and diving. 'Maybe ...' Mella paused as if uncertain of her own thoughts.

'Maybe ...' Anna prompted.

'Maybe I could get into the water with him the next time I come.'

Her friend grinned with delight: 'but you won't tell anyone that Cutty was here, will you?'

Mella nodded her assent. They stayed with Cutty for quite some time, watching him in silence, both spellbound by the ease and elegance of his movements, but Anna was in pensive mood. Maybe Caroline was right. She had just witnessed again the wonderful sense of wellbeing Cutty could generate in those who came in contact with him and maybe it would be selfish not to share precious moments like these with thousands of television viewers. Yet Cutty had to be protected. If only they could reach a compromise. These were the thoughts that kept her busy all the way home.

Mella was bubbling with excitement and bursting to share her good news with her mother; it would be all right to tell her mother about her meeting with Cutty in the cove, wouldn't it?

Anna nodded but still she was troubled that she could think of no way out of her own dilemma when it came to the television crew.

Her father, however, thought of a solution at supper time. 'Maybe you could play with the dolphin and go for a ride with him in the harbour,' he suggested. 'One or two people might get a bit of a shock but at least Cutty's visits to the cove would still be a secret and that's the most important thing, isn't it?'

'That's a great idea, Dad,' his daughter smiled 'but will it work? Won't Cutty be distracted by all the comings and goings of the fishing boats and the tourists?'

'Not if you pick a quiet time, very early in the morning or very late in the evening. The harbour is as quiet as the cove at those times,' her father assured her. Anna smiled happily; his suggestion seemed to be the perfect solution and she was sure it would appeal to Caroline too.

Tadhg's poaching companion Eamonn sometimes went diving too, for though he often made fine speeches about 'the fat cats trying to get rich quick on the back of the dolphin', he himself had fallen victim to the lure of the Spanish gold that might be buried somewhere amongst the scattered remnants of the *San Juan*. Donal had not been deterred by his frightening experience when he had suffered cramp but he had, however, abandoned all hopes of finding any treasure. But then he was like that, as Tom knew only too well: Donal's enthusiasm for a project lasted a week or two at best. The expert divers hired by the County Council had come to the conclusion that there was very little chance that gold would be found about the wreck of the galleon. How they had come to that conclusion they did not say but they seemed to know what they were talking about. Donal's interest in the gold, however, began to wane the moment Cutty had come to his rescue and quite apart from the notoriety he had gained from telling his story about that unique experience, quite apart from the discouraging views of the experts, there was now another very pleasant distraction. Caroline Mason wanted to do a few pencil sketches of him before she began to depict on canvas an imaginative portrayal of how Cutty had helped to support him in the water. The frivolous but likeable Donal was only too happy to co-operate. So very early next morning as Donal prepared to set out for Caroline's studio there were only two divers in the water off Claddaheen, diving separately. One of them was Eamonn, the other was Tom who was a member of the local historical society and had been asked to give a talk about his dives at their monthly meeting. Two medals, two plates, a shattered scent bottle and a few battered bowls and tankards were all that had been found to date.

The morning was misty, the waters clouded and grey as Tom swam above the widely scattered planks, unaware of the second diver's presence. He lingered above one of the planks for a few moments, remembering what he had read about the *San Juan*. It had been carvel-built, its hull formed of planks made flush at the seams. It had been a three-masted sailing ship, square rigged on the main and foremasts, lateen rigged, that is bearing a triangular sail on the mizzen mast, the third mast from the bow. What a marvel of construction it must have been, slender and graceful, the forecastle where the crew was quartered streamlined into the hull behind a projection called the beak head, heavy timbers or waist trees in the waist of the ship and brightly coloured canvas stretched about the waist to prevent the crew men from being seen by enemy bowmen and musketeers. The historical society was planning to set up a small local museum in the old Protestant church which had been kindly donated, and the finds from the *San Juan* would surely take pride of place amongst the exhibits. Tom had brought along an underwater camera — an expensive camera which he had hired in Tralee — and soon he began to take some photographs of the rotting planks and the sea bed around them. The photos would be very useful when he gave his talk to the society, though it was a prospect he did not relish, for unlike Donal he was not an exhibitionist. He took shots from various angles, desperately hoping that the images would be reasonably well defined when the photographs were developed. Conditions were less than perfect, but then he had the use of the camera for only a day or two.

Suddenly his attention was attracted to a crab scuttling about on the sea bed. His eyes followed the crab for a moment but then almost instinctively returned to the spot where the crab had emerged from amongst a cluster of stones. And there it was: a faint glimmer in the water, a golden glimmer. Tom's heart began to throb and he moved quickly towards the trembling shimmer. Was it possible that he was about to discover a hoard of golden coins? When he reached out his hand towards the faint light, his fingers came in contact not with a circular coin but with the links of a small chain. He tugged gently at it, gently, gently, gently; it would be terrible if he damaged it in some way, his movements encumbered by the weight of the camera about his neck. Little clouds of silt began to swirl about the chain which made it still more difficult for the diver to see, and yet there was no doubt in his mind that the chain was made of gold. It seemed to be so firmly embedded in the stones that it would never budge, but at last he pulled it free. His eyes shone with delight for there, dangling at the end of the chain, was a magnificent golden bird, and it seemed to be studded with precious jewels.

His heart drummed with greater intensity than before for he could scarcely believe that he was really holding a fabulous Spanish pendant.

Tom did not know it but the eyes of Eamonn 'the weasel' were upon him. Then without warning Eamonn lunged at him from behind, placing his left hand about Tom's neck and struggling with his right hand to wrench the precious pendant from his grasp. The surprise attack, like that of a shark on a lone herring, stunned Tom. He felt the fingers pressing tightly about his throat. Eamonn's face wore a distorted grimace of determination behind his face mask, his round brown eyes shining with greed. The pendant would be his passport to a new tomorrow.

Tom struggled to break free but he could not shake off his unseen attacker's stranglehold upon him — and yet he clung to the golden chain with the tenacity of a crab. He would not surrender it to anyone. When the numbness of the initial shock began to dissipate, Tom jerked his right elbow backwards, hitting his attacker in the stomach and causing him to lose concentration for a moment. He kicked backwards with his legs too. Eamonn's grip on his victim's throat was beginning to loosen and he tumbled to the right, but it was only a momentary respite for Tom, for seconds later Eamonn had fallen upon him again with renewed intensity. Now they grappled with one another, kicking and punching with all their might. Bubbles of froth winked about them and occasional clouds of silt rose from the silent world beneath them. Tom could not clearly see his attacker's face, but he sensed the resolution and grimness which gave such powers to his attacker's onslaught.

Tom's responses, however, were impeded by the heavy camera about his neck. It was not long before the thrashing of the underwater combat attracted a curious onlooker. Cutty lingered in the distance for a little while as if waiting for the right moment to make his move.

That moment finally came when Tom lashed out at his attacker with a violent kick and sent him shooting backwards through the water. The dolphin came zooming towards the hapless Eamonn, jerking him from below, and before he knew it his legs were spread wide apart across the new-comer's head and he was being whizzed through the water at incredible speed. Eamonn was astounded and terrified; he was scarcely aware of what was happening to him; all he knew was that he was hurtling through the grey of the tide, his body like a piece of driftwood swept hither and thither in a raging sea. But Cutty was merely taking him for a ride, a ride he would never forget. It was as if the man's entire being were powered by some hidden source of energy as the super-smooth body of the dolphin cruised through the tide.

Tom could only guess what had happened too; he had seen the dolphin surging towards them but what he had done with his attacker he did not know. Like a fine-skinned submarine the dolphin sped silently through the still greyness of the water, his passenger still astride his head. That passenger had never been so overcome with fear in all his life. The ride did not last very long but to Eamonn it seemed as if it would never end. The great bulk of the mighty dolphin lay beneath him and yet there was not the slightest hint of turbulence or resistance in the water. If the ride had been offered in a spirit of playful exuberance it would have been an experience to treasure, but Cutty's movements were determined and pur-poseful: he was taking Tom's aggressor further and further away from the scene of the attack. Seconds later he dumped him unceremoniously like so much flotsam on the tide. Eamonn was sent hurtling forwards face down, the water foaming white about him, but though he was shocked and trembling he had suffered no real injury. Cutty swam back towards Tom, humping and diving about him as if he were elated at the knowledge that he himself had saved the day and that his friend was unharmed.

The trauma of the attack could not be readily shaken off, but blended with Tom's feelings of terror and dismay was a feeling of triumph, for he had made the discovery of a life-time. The discovery would not distract the limelight from the gallant Cutty as might have been expected for he had made himself part of the discovery too. And Tom was yet another who had reason to be grateful that the beautiful warm-hearted dolphin had chosen to make his home in the waters about Claddaheen.

CHAPTER EIGHT

By mid-August, Anna's dolphin diary had many more entries. The identity of Tom's attacker remained a mystery but the handsome Cutty had again won the admiration of everyone, especially the residents of the village and the townland of Claddaheen. The dolphin's intelligence was discussed over and over again. Tom's discovery, the magnificent golden pendant, was the subject of much discussion too. The pendant took the form of a pelican and was both enamelled and studded with an almandine, diamonds and pearls. Several photographs had been taken of it and it had been sent to Dublin for special cleaning. Later it was hoped it would be installed in a place of honour in the new museum in the Protestant church.

The television crew was now in Claddaheen, filming sequences of Anna and Cutty out in the bay very early in the morning as Anna's father had suggested. The girl with the light blonde hair and bright blue eyes sat in the inflatable boat playing tunes for her friend on the tin whistle, while the dolphin leaped and danced. Translucent droplets cascaded from the silver arch of his body that seemed to hang suspended in the air for a moment or two before disappearing beneath the surface once more.

The crew were amazed at Cutty's frolics, for not only did he enjoy the music but he also seemed to appreciate changes in tempo from one tune to the next. When the rhythm was jaunty and lilting the dolphin was in boisterous mood, leaping from the water with explosive bursts of energy. When the music mellowed he became less exuberant, more relaxed, arching and circling with an elegance and poise that belied his enormous mass. The rosy light of the morning sun lent the film sequence an enchanted fairytale quality.

The crew remained at a distance from the scene of the action for some time, the cameraman focusing on the dolphin and the girl with a powerful zoom lens. Whenever there was a pause in the music Cutty popped his head through the water and hung in a vertical position, his beautiful eyes glinting in the sunlight. His eyes were filled with curiosity — it was as if he were wondering what had caused the interruption.

Soon Anna joined him in the water, but at first Cutty seemed more interested in the cameraman who had taken his place in the water too. The cameraman was a newcomer and Cutty was fascinated by new people. For some time he bumped and prodded the cameraman from behind before swimming round to face him directly, then gazing at close quarters into the lens of the camera. The cameraman remained perfectly still and the dolphin soon concluded that his old friend Anna was much more fun for she began to tease him by rattling the sweet-tin lids on a string beneath the water. One of the film crew had suggested throwing a ball to Cutty to see if he would play with it but Anna had objected

— even though Cutty liked to make people happy he was not a performing animal and so the idea of the ball had been promptly abandoned. Cutty and Anna played about in the water for some time and again the film crew were amazed that a wild creature of the deep could show such trust and such confidence in humankind.

Soon it seemed as if Cutty had become so absorbed in his frolics with Anna that he was completely unaware of the presence of the cameraman. What magnificent curling and curving he indulged in! How lissome and lithe his body! It was as if the presence of the girl and the bond of friendship between them invigorated him with a still deeper zest for life. A light sea breeze caressed his skin, splashes of spume rising and falling when he leapt and dived. Anna moved closer and stroked his body with the soft and velvety paintbrush bristles that had given her her first moment of indirect contact with his body. Cutty clearly enjoyed the sensation of those gentle strokes for he gently flicked the flukes of his enormous tail up and down. Anna sometimes wondered if the softness of the bristles tickled him, but then it was difficult to tell for Cutty always had such smiling eyes. Then she abandoned the brush and rubbed his right side with her fingers as he hung almost motionless beside her relishing the soothing touch of those fingers. He liked a gentle scratch too for though he might sometimes dart to the right or to the left he always returned for a repeat performance.

Then came the moment of moments when Anna took a firm hold of his dorsal fin and he took her for a ride about the rose-tinted harbour, the sunlight gilding the slopes of the hills across the bay. It was only at times like this that Anna fully appreciated the dolphin's boundless energy and power; only at times like this that she fully grasped something of the harmony between them. There were gasps of amazement from those on board the film boat; they had seen dolphins perform in dolphinariums in Britain and America, taught to adjust their behaviour patterns to a series of bribes and rewards, but what was so wonderful about Cutty and Anna was that he was wild and free while she offered him no inducement — other than the warmth of her friendship — to behave in a certain way. It would make the most spectacular footage, they enthused, as their gaze followed the dolphin and girl round and round the bay. If Cutty had learned to trust Anna she had learned to trust him too, and so the exhilaration of the ride was not tainted by fear or alarm: she knew Cutty was her friend and he would do nothing to harm her. She wished the ride could go on and on and on, for it seemed as if they were the only two creatures alive in the whole wide world.

When she saw how pleased the film crew were with what they had witnessed, Anna decided to sing a song she had written in honour of her very special friend. Much to her delight the crew liked it and one of them set it to music. Two days later she sang her song into the tape recorder for the sound-track of the film:

Wild dolphin, wild dolphin can I be your friend,
Where the fun has no end,
In your kingdom so joyful and free?

Wild dolphin, wild dolphin, can I be your friend,
When you ride like the wind,
Through the green and the blue of the sea?

Wild dolphin, wild dolphin, can I be close by
When you leap through the sky
And the sun blazes warm on your skin?

The song was a lovely simple song, the crew members said, and Anna sang it beautifully. It would really be a spectacular programme, they assured her.

Then they interviewed Donal who told yet again how Cutty had saved his life, and the story seemed to be embellished with some new little detail at every telling. Next came an interview with Tom whose account of how the dolphin had whisked away his attacker at high speed was more factual but none the less fascinating for those who heard it. They talked to some of the boatmen who explained what a difference the coming of the dolphin had made to their lives, especially since the fishing season was proving to be such a disaster. Many of them might have had to emigrate, they said, were it not for the boisterous Cutty, but now they were ferrying boatloads of visitors out to see the dolphin several times a day. Shopkeepers and pub owners were interviewed too. Dolly from the craft shop, told how a number of local craftsmen and women had been inspired by the dolphin, as she showed sweaters and tee-shirts with dolphin motifs, souvenirs carved from bog oak in the form of dolphins, dolphin jewellery, dolphin pottery, dolphin glassware, dolphin prints, photographs and postcards. A special section of the programme would be devoted to Caroline Mason and her paintings, some of which she had hurriedly framed for the occasion, and of course she played a tune on the fiddle for them in the living-room of her cottage.

Though Mella now had no difficulty in getting into a boat and though she'd had several encounters with the dolphin in Anna's secret cove, she had not as yet ventured into the water with Cutty. Caroline decided that the coming of the film-makers might be just the spur she needed to tempt her into doing so. And so it was that one fine morning in mid-August Mella gingerly edged into the water, Anna by her side, the cameraman on board a boat a little distance away. Mella recalled how her fingers had fleetingly come into contact with Cutty's skin when, urged on by Anna, she had reached out and touched his head. It had been the most exciting sensation she had ever experienced. Now as he came towards her in the water, her heart was pulsating with excitement. Anna had told her not to be afraid if he bumped and prodded her with his beak; he meant no harm; that was simply his way of investigating her as best he could. Soon Cutty was engaged in a little gentle bumping, precisely as Anna had predicted, but then he began to swim around her. Her deep brown eyes shone with delight and when she touched him it was like touching her most beautiful dream.

Now they would have more than enough footage for a complete programme about Cutty. When the programme was shown later in the year it would not only be a further boost for the local tourist industry, it would also — and more importantly — portray the impact the dolphin had made on the lives of the people who lived in Claddaheen summer and winter. It would depict in a special way the dolphin's unique relationship with five very different people: the sensitive Anna, the timid Mella, the frivolous Donal, the more serious but good-humoured Tom and the artistic Caroline. It would be a wonderful film, a celebration of all the goodness and joy that the dolphin had inspired and continued to inspire. There would be a special preview in the local cinema in a few months' time before the programme was transmitted on TV. Eamonn, however, resented the arrival of the film makers almost as much as he resented the presence of the dolphin and he was therefore more than happy when they departed. As he stood on the strand mending the nets one morning, the dazzle of sunlight on water hurting his eyes, his poaching partner Tadhg came walking briskly towards him. Eamonn had been bitterly disappointed when he had been unable to get his hands on that old Spanish pendant; it must be worth a small fortune. Of course he had told no one, not even Tadhg, of his attack on Tom but now he bore an even deeper grudge against the dolphin, for the dolphin had not only ruined the fishing season and put their poaching escapades at risk, he had also robbed him of that priceless pendant.

'A penny for your thoughts,' the stern-faced Tadhg said when he drew near.

'I was thinking that only a fool would believe there was no more gold out there with the wreck,' Eamonn replied, mending a tear in the meshes that he conveniently blamed on the dolphin.

'Maybe there is,' the other mused, 'but it isn't much use to you or me if we can't lay our hands on some of it.' He eyed his companion suspiciously, for Eamonn had some pretty devious notions at times.

'A few sticks of dynamite here and there would shake things up,' Eamonn smirked.

'No, no,' Mella's stepfather retorted. 'Much too risky.'

'Divil the risk,' the man at the net assured him. 'Who knows what might be thrown up and with a bit of luck we might be able to kill two birds with one stone.'

Tadhg looked at him curiously — he did not understand.

'With a bit of luck that dolphin might meet his Waterloo when the dynamite went off, for he's as inquisitive as Nora the Cross,' Eamonn explained, 'and even if he didn't get hurt at all a few good loud bangs might be enough to frighten him off for good.'

This latter idea appealed to Tadhg who really believed that the coming of the dolphin was an omen of bad luck which explained the small catches by the fishing boats.

Within a week, Eamonn had managed to get his hands on

some dynamite, and at five o'clock one morning he was diving in the water above the grave of the *San Juan*. The sky was beginning to brighten but the vast expanse of the bay was slumbering and still — not even the squawk of a gull disturbed the stillness. Tadhg waited in a boat some distance away — an expression of grim intensity in his hazel eyes. Eamonn set the charges one by one, most of them not too far from the precise location where Tom had discovered the pendant, and as he predicted it was only a matter of moments before the curious Cutty appeared on the scene. The dolphin eyed the action of the diver intently — he was intrigued by all kinds of activity. Eamonn looked at the creature anxiously for a moment — surely he was not preparing to jerk him onto his head and take him for another terrifying ride around the bay? But Cutty had no such thoughts this time. He just swam about, veering to the right and to the left, disappearing for a few moments only to reappear in some different quarter a little later. Yet there was a sense of urgency in the diver's movement. All the charges were set to explode at 5.15 and now the minute hand reached seven minutes past five, the second hand moving relentlessly forwards all the while. Cutty was in great danger now for though there were only a few sticks of dynamite in each charge, he would certainly be killed or badly injured if he came too close to any of them when they exploded. The water was very clear, but Eamonn's field of vision beneath the waves was fairly limited and he could see nothing in the middle distance save a blue-green haze that heaved to and fro with a gentle swell.

When he had placed his last charge, Eamonn swam back towards the boat. He had scarcely clambered aboard when he noticed a high fin protruding from the water. At first he thought it was the fin of the dolphin but then the dolphin leapt high in the air above the grave of the *San Juan* and

Eamonn shivered. It was surely the fin of a porbeagle shark. Most people said they were harmless to man and yet the very sight of their ominous fins filled the fishermen with dread. He had seen a porbeagle shark dead on a strand a few years before and had marvelled at its massive mouth and gill slits as well as its large triangular teeth with the small side cusps. Now the huge porbeagle cruised through the water with its dorsal fin and tail tip clearly visible. Eamonn clenched his fists in frustration and banged them together; there was no way he was getting in to the water while that shark was around and if the explosives alerted anyone in the village he would have no opportunity to explore the site to see if anything of value had been uncovered. The two men stood and watched intently, the minute hand on Eamonn's watch moving slowly, slowly, slowly to twelve minutes past five.

It was then that Cutty became aware of the presence of the newcomer. He eyed him intently as he swam a little distance from him. The shark was an intruder who had violated his territory. Of course he often escorted the fishing boats and the tourist boats in and out of his territory but they never stayed very long and they posed no threat for they were not his own kind. He saw the intimidating jaws of the shark and its powerful tail which boasted an extra ridge above and below the main side keel. They swam about each other for a few moments. The shark veered to the right; it appeared as if he were retreating without a fight when suddenly he lunged at the dolphin, opening his jaws to reveal those lethal teeth and flicking his tail from side to side at a frantic pace, churning the water and flecking it with curls of foam. Dolphin and shark thrashed and splashed in the water, swirls of spume seething around them, but it was difficult for the men on the boat to see precisely what was happening.

'Bad luck to them, that they wouldn't have their fight

somewhere else,' Mella's stepfather moaned.

'Maybe that shark is doing us a service by keeping the dolphin just where we want him,' his companion retorted, now convinced that if the intruder survived the blast he would swim away to safety the moment the explosion occurred. Cutty tried to make an attack from the right or the left flank, to ram the majestic shark in the side with his powerful beak but the wily shark always darted out of danger. Eamonn looked at his watch again and pursed his lips, and still the dolphin and the shark made hostile charges at one another, swerving and veering this way and that like boxers in a ring. The flicking of their tails generated more and more turbulence in the foaming water. Sometimes it seemed as if the voracious jaws of the shark would sink deep into Cutty's flesh and his noble blood would spurt forth from the wound, reddening the sea around them. Sometimes it seemed as if Cutty's powerful beak would crash against the intruder's side, the impact stunning the shark and rendering him unconscious so that he would plunge to the gloomy depths. But each was too keen, too alert, to allow his adversary to win the day. Suddenly the charges began to explode one by one, great fountains of spume shooting skywards all around, only to crash to the surface once more. Eamonn's smiling eyes focused on the bubbling cataracts of foam that rose and fell with such splendour and intensity. Seconds later the fountains had subsided; great swirls of spume were still seething on the tide but now both dolphin and shark had vanished without trace. Eamonn adjusted his face mask and dropped into the water once more, his heart pounding with anticipation. The explosions had been real beauties and it would be a great surprise to him if they had not thrown up something of value: a few coins, a few pieces of silverware, maybe another pendant or two, anything was possible.

He did not know that at that very moment the hapless shark was bleeding badly and was sinking to his doom on the stony sea bed. Cutty the wild dolphin of Claddaheen was nowhere to be seen.

CHAPTER NINE

Eamonn swam in the murky water, clouds of silt swirling about him. It would take longer than he had imagined for the silt to settle and the visibility was now so poor that he could only see a little distance in front of him. The explosions had, however, roused half the village and a crowd was already rushing towards the strand. What on earth had happened? they wondered anxiously, their footsteps hurried and urgent, their voices hushed and trembling. Had there been an explosion on board a boat? Was it possible that somebody had been injured or even killed? Tom's friend Donal was amongst the adventurous few who clambered into boats and made their way out into the bay, most of the others opting to remain on the strand once it had been established with the use of binoculars that there was no trace of wreckage on the tide. There was no time for Tadhg to row away so the only thing to be done was to make a pretence of fishing: luckily there was a small net lying in a tangle on the floor of the boat. Tadhg threw the net across the port side of the boat and when the other boats drew near they saw him apparently drawing the net into the boat once more.

'What happened?' someone called out to him.

He shrugged his shoulders to indicate that he did not know and did not care.

Had he seen where the explosions had taken place?

'Much further out,' he retorted with a sweep of his left hand.

Was it a coincidence that Mella's stepfather was fishing so close to the site of the *San Juan*, some few wondered secretly to themselves? Was it possible that he himself had had something to do with the explosion? For he seemed more than a little agitated even though he tried to convey the impression that the explosions were a matter of little consequence to him. Was he yet another who had succumbed to the lure of Spanish gold? Yet it did not seem plausible, for Tadhg did not know how to dive and the explosions had taken place underwater. Better to keep clear of the area for a little while longer in case there might be further explosions, someone else suggested and so it was with a sigh of relief that Tadhg observed the small flotilla of boats return to the shore, those on board still mystified by the strange events of the morning.

Meanwhile Eamonn swam about in the murky underwater haze, desperately hoping to uncover some Spanish treasure which would reward him for his efforts, but he became more and more frustrated with each passing second. There was nothing, nothing at all, just tiny remnants of the rotting planks that had fragmented when the dynamite had exploded and that were now strewn here, there and everywhere about the floor of the sea. There was anger and frustration in his round brown eyes; it had all been a complete waste of time! Yet he was determined to survey as much of the site as possible for he might not get a second chance and it would really be ironic if he overlooked some precious object disturbed by the explosion only for it to be discovered by some less deserving diver a few days later. Backwards and forwards he swam, gazing hawk-like, but try as he might he could not see a shimmering golden sheen that might betray the presence of a hoard of coins. Small rocks and stones had been flung hither and thither, abandoning their long established stations and coming to rest in new locations. If anything of value had been disturbed it had surely been buried again.

Eamonn remained in the water for a long time, slowly rising to the surface only when his supply of oxygen began to run dangerously low. He returned to the boat and struggled on board, Tadhg giving him a helping hand. He did not know that Donal Jones had his binoculars focused upon him. Donal could not identify the diver, and so he hoped against hope that he would remove his head gear. A few seconds later he obliged. Eamonn, the rancorous Eamonn! He might have known. And it had probably been Eamonn who had attacked Tom too, for Eamonn had been seething in the pub about the phoneys in the village pretending to be interested in history when all they really cared about was making a name for themselves. Tom was very keen on history and it was perfectly plain that Eamonn resented his popularity for Tom was also a great basketballer — he was the star of the local team and often coached young players. Donal had suspected Eamonn as the attacker from the very beginning and had shared these suspicions with Tom but of course Tom had said in his cautious way that suspicions were one thing and proof was quite another. What Donal was witnessing now was enough to convince him at least that his suspicions had been correct all along.

At about ten o'clock that morning Mella met Anna and told

her that Cutty had been seen in the water just before the explosion. He had been fighting with a shark and a few moments later there had been patches of blood on the tide. Anna was devastated. It was worse than when Cutty had been struck by the boat. Mella added that her stepfather had said that if the explosions had served no other purpose they had surely put an end to that jinx of a dolphin.

How could her uncle be so hard-hearted? Anna wondered. She tried not to cry. Cutty was a survivor, she told herself; he had recovered from the wound left by the boat and he would recover from this too.

Mella too was distressed and so it fell to Anna to comfort her. Mella had become deeply attached to the dolphin, especially since she had entered the water with him. Getting so close to the wonderful dolphin, touching him and rubbing him had been a magical experience, so magical that she had swum with him again a day later in the privacy of Anna's secret cove. Her confidence was slowly returning. She had even begun to talk of joining Tom's basketball coaching sessions, something she had always longed to do. If she lost the magic of her relationship with Cutty at such a crucial stage, she might begin to withdraw into herself once more. That was why Anna firmly assured her that Cutty had not been hurt, that he would come back, and in a sense the words were intended to reassure herself as much as her friend.

'Let's go down to the cove and play a few tunes,' Anna suggested. It would take their mind off things and there was a possibility that Cutty might come to them, she said more in hope than in confidence.

'Great idea,' Anna's father agreed. 'It's best not to sit and brood.' He stood by the old stone wall that fronted the flower garden and watched them cycle down to the cove. Not long afterwards he was joined by Tadhg who had come to ask if he had left a rope behind the day before — he had misplaced it and could not find it.

'You're an awful man to be wishing that dolphin dead when he's made such a wonderful change in that girl's life,' Anna's father began.

'Anna, you mean?' Tadhg said curiously, standing at the wall and turning his gaze towards the road that meandered down to the partially hidden cove.

'No, Mella,' his brother insisted. 'Can't you see the change in her this past while since she's been meeting Cutty in the cove below with Anna.'

Tadhg did not reply, but this revelation came as a great surprise to him, for Mella's mother had thought it best to keep their daughter's encounters with the dolphin a secret from her husband. She knew how much Tadhg disliked the dolphin and it would only spoil things for Mella if he made a fuss about her visits to the cove. 'So that's why she's had such a long face all morning,' Tadhg retorted eventually.

'I've a long face myself and I'm not ashamed of it, for it would be a bad blow to Claddaheen if anything happened to that dolphin,' his brother went on.

'That's true enough for the shopkeepers have been filling their tills in a big way since his lordship came to town,' the stern-faced man replied bitterly.

'Ah, that's just a small part of it,' Anna's father explained. 'There's never been such a buzz of excitement about the place, never such good feeling, never such spirit, and the dolphin has a lot to do with that.' He paused and strained his eyes towards the outer reaches of the cove but the girls were now completely hidden from view. 'There's a coming to- gether in the place, a feeling that if people work together they can get things done — like at the old church: they've started to do it up already and they're planning to open the museum the week the film is shown in the cinema.'

Tadhg was not impressed; his brother always had very odd notions and what had museums and films to do with real life?

'The coming of the dolphin has restored people's faith in themselves and you need look no further than Mella to see that,' Anna's father insisted. The two men made their way round the back of the house, to search for the fishing rope. It took them only a few moments to find it. Just as Tadhg was about to get behind the wheel once more, Anna came rushing up the road waving her arms with furious delight. Cutty had not been killed! He was in the cove! He was in the cove! She was so overcome with happiness that she scarcely noticed her uncle in the car. Seconds later her father and her uncle drove down to the strand. The brothers stood on the shore watching the girls splash about in the water with the dolphin.

The handsome Cutty had survived unscathed but the explosion had clearly unnerved him for at first he seemed distant and aloof, even when the girls played for him as they sat in Caroline's inflatable boat. But when the girls entered the water he came a little closer and soon he was making his usual leaps and dives. These were leaps and dives, not only of joy but also of relief for it was perfectly plain he knew just how close he had come to death. Mella and Anna could not know that their friend had seen the bleeding body of the shark lying helpless on the stony sea bed — an image that had filled him with dread.

Then the sky began to brighten and once more Cutty was invigorated by sun and brine and salt sea air, his acrobatics becoming more and more boisterous — surely his way of saying how happy he was to be alive.

Tadhg could hardly believe his eyes, for there was Mella splashing about like a seal in the water. Only a few weeks before she had absolutely resisted every cajolement to get into a boat, quite apart from swimming. Tadhg had in his own way made more than a few efforts to coax her into doing so, mainly for the sake of Mella's mother, for he truly loved that woman. It was for her sake that he put a rein on his temper when he was tempted to rail angrily at his stepdaughter, but his abrupt and curt manner made it difficult for him to show affection at the best of times.

He had wondered why Mella's resentment over putting down Rover had abated so quickly; he had wondered too why a few days before she had hinted that she no longer believed he had let her father drown on purpose. She had held fast to that distorted notion simply because she felt bitter that all the others in the boat had been saved while her father had drowned. She had been looking for someone to blame and at first she had been so resentful when Tadhg had married her mother — it was as if he were trying to fill her father's shoes — that she had seen fit to make him the culprit. Of course she had not expressed herself so plainly but she had made a gesture of reconciliation. Only now did he understand the reason for this welcome change; it was the dolphin!

Tadhg watched in amazement when the dolphin ceased his frolics and moved close to the girls, both of them stroking him and caressing his smooth, streamlined body with their fingers. It was very difficult for a man like Tadhg to admit that he might have been wrong, that there might have been a reason other than the presence of the dolphin for the poor fishing catches, for he had been reared in a household where the old superstitions always held sway. During the past few weeks he had looked all about him and had seen the good fortune that the dolphin had brought to the lives of many of the people of Claddaheen and in a selfish way he had resented that good fortune, believing that he himself shared no part in it. But maybe, just maybe, he had been wrong.

'Well is there any chance we'll make you a convert to the dolphin?' Anna's father asked after a long silence, 'for isn't Mella's laughter the best music you've heard in a long time?'

Tadhg did not reply, but his brother sensed that he was more than a little dumbfounded by what he was witnessing.

That evening Anna spent a long time writing in her diary, recounting the events of the day. Cutty remained in the cove for the next few days, Anna and Mella visiting him again and again. Both of them were confident that he would venture back into the wide expanse of the bay in the not too distant future. Some of the villagers, however, began to wonder if the magnificent dolphin had deserted them again as he seemed to have done once before.

When she was not down on the strand with Mella, Anna sometimes swept barefoot through the fields. The holidays were coming to a close and already a faint breath of autumn could be heard in the rustle of the wind through the leaves, the fading blue petals of the meadow crane's-bill tumbling to the ground. It had been the most wonderful summer, she told herself as she made a garland of tufted vetch with its long racemes of purple pea-like flowers, interspersed here and there with the clustered yellow blossoms of the meadow vetchling. Sometimes a fine veil of mist drifted in from the sea and Anna loved romping through the mist, her father's cows grazing contentedly about her. Her mother often scolded her for being out in the mist, telling her she would surely catch her death of cold. Anna was a bit like the cows, her father asserted, for she also seemed to think that the mist, being perfectly natural, could be nothing but wholesome and good. If only the summer could last forever! And yet the blue-black swallows were already congregating on the telephone wires which they always did before setting out on their long, long journeys to sunnier climes.

Everyone seemed reasonably happy in the townland of Claddaheen. Mella and Tadhg were getting on much better and Mella went lobster fishing with her stepfather one day for the very first time in her life. It proved to be an awkward experience for both of them; they did not know what to say to each other, but at least it was a beginning.

One person, however, who was more than a little disgruntled was Eamonn King; he was sick and tired of Claddaheen where there was nothing but small minds and small dreams. Apart from the greedy few, the fat cats whose only goal in life was more and more money, most of the people had no ambition and no vision; their pathetic lives were ordinary, humdrum, monotonous; they found security in the same old drab routines, the only thing that added spice to their lives was a regular helping of gossip. Anyone who tried to be the least bit different was viewed with suspicion or scorn or ridicule. Luckily he was getting out soon and going to England.

It was thoughts such as these which flitted in and out of Eamonn's mind as he ambled down the street late one evening, and who should he see making his way towards his red sports car but Donal Jones. Donal had a date in Tralee and was dressed up in his beige linen suit and smart tie. Eamonn could not resist the temptation to shout 'Show-off!' at the owner of the sports car who fumbled for the keys in his trousers pocket.

At first Donal chose to ignore him, for though Eamonn huffed and puffed like the big bad wolf he could turn quite nasty at times. He had surely attacked Tom and he had surely planted those explosives which had caused such havoc at the *San Juan*. 'Living off your da!' Eamonn jeered again.

'Better than being a poacher!' Donal retorted.

'Well at least I'm not a scavenger like yourself and your

father,' the other smirked, drawing nearer and pushing Donal backwards with his strong right hand.

'It was you attacked Tom in the water that time wasn't it?' accused Donal. 'And I bet you caused the explosion too!'

'You watch your mouth,' snarled Eamonn. 'Where's your proof?' Without waiting for an answer he aimed a punch at Donal's jaw.

The two of them began to grapple, kicking and punching with all the determination they could muster. Donal had spent a great deal of time dressing and grooming himself before the mirror, but now his appearance was a matter of little consequence as he landed crashing blows against his opponent's face and upper body. Eamonn's face was puffed, his teeth gritted tightly together. The heavy thud of Eamonn's clenched fist fell against Donal's chest again and again but he would not give way. They fell to the ground, gasping and panting. A small cut opened below Eamonn's left eye and blood began to trickle from it. A few passers-by stopped to watch but they did not intervene. Eamonn grasped his opponent by the hair and bashed the back of his head against the car door, forcing Donal to shake his head vigorously from side to side to recover his senses. He could feel the sting of Eamonn's nails reaching for his face. His own hands now gripped Eamonn's neck. Droplets of sweat glistened on Eamonn's gnarled forehead and on his thinning blonde hair, as his sweaty fingers caught hold of the other's cheeks and twisted them out of shape. Just when it seemed as if Eamonn would gain the upper hand, Donal jerked his knee upwards, stabbing it against his opponent's paunchy stomach. Eamonn gave a painful grunt, loosening his grasp on the other's cheeks. The contest was over but they lay beside the car grunting and groaning for a little while. Then Donal struggled to his feet, wiping the blood from his lips and wearily stumbling against the bonnet of the car for a moment. His body was sweaty all over, his clothes wrinkled and grimy. He would have to wash and change and make a quick phone call before driving to Tralee.

Eamonn rested his head against the wheel of the car, eyeing his departing opponent grimly. Now he was more determined than ever that he would not leave Claddaheen without giving Donal and his likes a parting gift. And what better gift than a battered and bloodied dolphin?

CHAPTER TEN

Late one evening, Anna snorkelled and splashed in the waters of the cove with Cutty, but they were not alone. Lurking somewhere in the blue-green underwater haze was a diver — a diver with a knife in his hands, its blade long and tapering.

Cutty's frolics never ceased to amaze his companion. His curling and curving, arching and circling were all so spontaneous and yet his movements were so elegant, so beautiful they might have been choreographed by a ballet dancer. When he leapt from the water there was a flash of silver and grey, the graceful sweep of his back and the gleaming sheen of his belly suspended for a second in the air. Cutty really was a dancer, for he danced to the music of wind and wave. No one could really own such a joyful dolphin for he was a free spirit, and yet Anna still regarded him as her dolphin in a very special way. She had been the first to greet him and since that day in May they had spent so much time together, shared so many experiences. Because of him she would be seen by thousands of people when the television programme was screened. She had received a postcard from the film-makers telling her that the editing had now been completed.

Now, having indulged in much frolicking and leaping, Cutty remained quietly in the water beside Anna. She did not speak to him at times such as this, did not even whisper, for just being together, so close and so secure, was all the communication they needed. She felt proud that he had chosen to seek refuge in the secret cove after the explosion, even though he now ventured back into the wider bay from time to time. Ribbons of gold languished on the tide — a secret cove, a girl and a dolphin, a wonderful dream. Then, suddenly, the illusion of perfect happiness was shattered. A dark shadow came sweeping through the water. Anna's bright blue eyes widened in horror when she saw the ominous silver flash of the deadly blade. The drama lasted only a few seconds but Anna seemed to see it in horrific slow motion. In a moment of undiluted horror she saw the massive blade thrust at the dolphin's side with a strength born of enmity and malice. It was Eamonn's hand which gave impetus to the knife as it sliced through the water but Anna could only focus on the blade itself, a blade aimed to destroy the dream and the beauty and spatter it with blood.

Impulsively she lunged at the handle of the stabbing blade. Its sharp edge slit the flesh at the top of her thumb and blood like red dye began to spurt from the wound. The sudden movement roused the dolphin from his lethargy, for he had been lulled into a false sense of security by the swell and the sunlight and the soft sea breeze. He dived and disappeared. The girl struggled to remove the knife from Eamonn's grasp but the grip of those stubby fingers was firm and strong. She could see the anger in his round brown eyes that glared at her from behind his face mask. His gaze filled her with fear but still she grappled with the stubby fingers, while Eamonn menacingly jerked the blade towards her face. Then he reached out and grabbed her with his unrestrained left hand, holding her firm by his side. Where was the dolphin? Eamonn wondered grimly. He was still close by, he was sure of that. Maybe the sound of his companion's distress — the vibrations of her splashing and thrashing with her legs — would summon him back to the scene of the drama. Anna struggled to get free but her captor would not release his hold upon her. She fought to breathe evenly through the tube of her snorkel that projected above the water. Then suddenly the beak of the dolphin reappeared in the hazy distance. Anna felt so helpless; she knew what the wily Eamonn had in mind; he was using her as bait to tempt Cutty nearer to him. The sight of that monstrous blade sent shivers of despair tingling down her spine.

Cutty humped and arched about them for a few moments as if wondering what to do. Then he came and hung almost motionless a little distance before them. It was as if he were still debating with himself; he could not ram Eamonn with his beak for then he would surely cause serious injury to Anna too. Oh how she wished that Cutty would swim away; she willed him to do so with every fibre of her being. She would never forgive herself if anything happened to the wonderful wild dolphin that had enriched her life and made her feel so special. She looked at that beautiful beak and those smiling eyes — if only she knew precisely what he was thinking. Who could tell what would happen if Cutty made a sudden reckless onslaught against his aggressor? And yet she felt that he was too intelligent, too perceptive to attempt anything rash. The waiting seemed endless but then suddenly Cutty vanished from view again. Was he swimming out of danger's way? Had he come to the conclusion that retreat was the wisest course of action? Again the seconds seemed to drag like hours for Eamonn did not release his grip, clearly believing that the dolphin was somewhere nearby.

Seconds later a thunderous splash of water flooded Anna's ears as Cutty lashed the massive flukes of his tail against Eamonn's back. Anna was shaken free and went spinning down and down, bubbles gurgling explosively in the voluminous wash of water that followed in the wake of that mighty tail. For a split second she could see her father's face before her and her mother calling to her with lips that did not speak. She saw strange undulating silent images of the black cows grazing in the evening mist, but then the mellow mist became darker and denser, the water colder and blacker. She began to feel cold, so cold.

She did not know that Eamonn was plummeting downwards too a little distance away. She struggled frantically, almost involuntarily with her hands, kicking with her legs, hearing a strange deafening oozing in her ears. There seemed no hope when suddenly her groping fingers found a massive fin and she was lifted gently, slowly upwards towards the surface. The undulating swell became lighter and greener again, shafts of sunlight rippling here and there. Cutty, gallant Cutty had not abandoned her.

When her head broke the surface once more she spurted the brine from her mouth — it seemed to spew from the very depths of her throat — and wiped her dripping hair away from her eyes. She gasped and gasped, her heart pounding with terrible intensity. She had never known such fear, but now she sighed with relief when she saw the beautiful Cutty circling about her. She struggled towards the inflatable. Eamonn had surely been injured; she would have to go and get help. But she had scarcely reached the strand when her father came running towards her. He had been ambling down the hill and had sensed that something was wrong when he could see no trace of herself or the dolphin. 'Eamonn! Eamonn! Eamonn's in the water,' she gasped, but then they saw the diver spluttering and coughing at the scene of the drama. He had received a stunning flick of the tail against his back but the dolphin had not injured him. Anna's father fussed and fretted over her. She assured him that she was perfectly all right now but he insisted that he would telephone the doctor the moment they returned to the house. He looked at her bloodied finger. He would telephone the police too, he went on, as he placed his arm about her and led her away from the strand. Eamonn had gone too far this time.

'No police, Dad, no police,' Anna pleaded with a vigour that surprised him. 'I think he's learned his lesson.'

'The sad fact is that there are some people who never learn their lesson,' her father replied but he did not wish to quarrel with her now.

'Cutty has been great for Claddaheen,' the girl went on, 'and it would spoil everything if the police were dragged in.'

Her father told her to rest and to forget about Eamonn; she must take things easy for a while. Perhaps she was right though, for now that Eamonn had been identified he would surely be very slow to make an attack on the dolphin again. He knew that if he did he would bring the wrath of the entire population down upon his head. Besides, he had already booked his ticket to England.

The holidays were coming to an end and so Anna spent more time than ever with Cutty in the cove. She was sometimes joined by Mella and Caroline who adored him as much as she did. She wrote in her diary too with the same enthusiasm as before, committing to paper her feelings about the dolphin, feelings that she would not readily share with anyone else — and she took great pleasure from flicking through the pages in quiet moments and reading over incidents that had happened a few weeks or a few months before.

And yet a nagging, niggling feeling of uncertainty strayed into her mind from time to time. Cutty had become a little more aloof, more remote, more distant again. Was this a consequence of Eamonn's attack or was there some other reason of which she was unaware? At the same time, he often seemed as boisterous and as playful as ever.

She told Caroline her thoughts one morning as they stood in the converted interior of the old Protestant church which would have to be fitted with an elaborate security system before the magnificent golden pendant from the *San Juan* would go on display — and even then it would not be on permanent display. The church museum was to be officially opened in late September with a special showing of Caroline's dolphin paintings. Now the artist and her friend stood beneath the handsome stained glass window in the eastern gable that looked towards the sea, dazzling morning light spilling across the old slated flags that formed the floor. Much of the work of conversion had now been completed and Caroline was trying to decide where individual paintings might be hung to best advantage. Her most recent work was a painting of Mella and Cutty. In another fantasy work she had been unable to resist the temptation of painting Cutty with the fabulous Spanish pendant dangling from his neck. Anna laughed when she saw it, for Cutty had been depicted as a winsome rogue with an eye for ancient treasures. Now Anna talked to Caroline about Cutty's apparent aloofness. The artist herself had not noticed it, but then Anna was much more sensitive about such things. 'Dolphins have their moods like the rest of us, I expect,' she said in an effort to reassure her friend, 'and the attack must surely have made some impact on him.'

'If I could be sure that it was just the attack it wouldn't be so bad because Cutty's trust in humans will grow again with time,' Anna replied in pensive mood, 'but I have a feeling there is something else.'

'What else could there be?' her companion wondered with characteristic earnestness. 'Or might it simply be that Cutty's hearing the call of the wild, luring him back to his own kind again.' She stood beneath a side window and paused, assessing for a moment which of her paintings might be most suitable for this particular position. 'Wild dolphins, even when they are as friendly as Cutty, do not stay very long in one place.'

'Maybe you're right,' Anna replied still unconvinced, 'but it's kind of like when a person you know well behaves a bit differently towards you and you can't understand why.'

One wet September evening, Anna made her way down to the cove after school, looking out for Cutty as usual. There was no sign of him. Spirals of clouds like great black swirls trailed helplessly across the brooding sky. The water was cooler now and she did not venture into it but she stood on the beach and played the tin whistle. Still Cutty did not come. She wanted him to be free to make his own choices; she hoped that he would never lose that freedom and yet this did not lessen the pangs of sadness that tugged at her heart-strings now. Caroline was surely right. Cutty had probably decided it was time to be with his own kind again, but it would have made her feel better to have bid him a tender goodbye and wished him well in his new adventures.

Her father and mother consoled her when she returned to the farmhouse on the hill. Cutty might be back the next day, her father suggested, but even if he were not they must try to look at things from his point of view. Just as humans needed human friends, so a dolphin needed dolphin friends. They must be grateful that he had chosen to spend some time with them, and given them so many precious memories. How many people in Ireland, in the world indeed, could boast of such magical moments with a wild and beautiful dolphin?

An hour or so later Anna wrote in her diary again. Cutty had not come to her and oh how empty and desolate the cove seemed without his boisterous leaping and diving! If he were somewhere new was he thinking of her now? Would he ever think of her again?

That night Anna's dreams were filled with images of the marvellous magical Cutty and she relived again some of the moments of exuberance and tenderness they had shared together. Cutty did not come the next day nor the day after that and Anna found it more and more difficult to concentrate at school. She was constantly day-dreaming and the teacher only made matters worse by reminding her that the summer was over now. Maybe the summer was over but the warmth and the magic still lingered in her heart. She could not banish the sadness or the sense of regret when she came to write a new entry in her diary each evening. The questions haunted her. Where had Cutty gone and why had he chosen to leave at this particular time? It would be so terrible if her dolphin diary had to end with this kind of uncertainty.

Of course she still tramped the misty fields to herd home the cows for milking in the evening; she still listened to the plaintive whistle of the plover and the liquid twitter of the goldfinch; she still plucked wild flowers in field and hedge-row — the tiny packed blossoms of the pink self-heal and the violet-blue bells of the pretty harebell — but still she longed, oh how she longed to see the graceful Cutty humping through the water.

At long last, very early on a Saturday morning in late September she rose and went to the window, and there at the outer edge of the cove was a dolphin indulging in the most boisterous leaping and diving. Cutty! Cutty! He was back, he was back! Her heart began to dance again as she hurriedly donned her clothes, slipped downstairs, grabbed her tin whistle and cycled towards the strand. The morning was cool and fresh, the rush of the wind catching her long hair and making it stream about her shoulders, and yet she did not feel cold for she had only one thought now and that was of Cutty's return. There was no buzz of car or lorry from the road above as she followed the meandering coil that took her to the strand at last. Caroline had been talking about stowing away her inflatable for safe keeping for the wintertime but luckily it was still on the strand. Anna pushed it into the water, leapt on board and began to row with all the strength she could muster. She was still a considerable distance from the dolphin but she held her gaze upon him.

There was something unusual, something which intrigued her, though she did not know precisely what it might be. All she knew was that Cutty had scarcely dived through the greeny blue of the tide when a split second later he was arching through the air once more. The interval between the dive and the leap seemed incredibly short for it was generally no more than a second, and that was strange for Cutty generally liked to roll and curl beneath the water for a few moments before zooming like a rocket through the surface yet again. Was Cutty feeling even more exhilarated than usual? Or could it be that ...? She rowed nearer and nearer to the scene of the exuberant frolics where explosive bursts of spray were rising like geysers. Then her eyes widened with joy and delight. Yes, yes, her first impression had been correct: there was not one dolphin in the water but two! The light began to glisten in her eyes again. Her very own Cutty had found a mate and now the two of them were dancing a boisterous ballet of love. She felt so happy for them. If Cutty had ever been lonely he would never be so again. The happiness the two wild dolphins shared radiated all around. And Cutty was more than pleased to hump playfully about the girl in the inflatable and in this manner tempting his less confident mate to do likewise. Anna could see that the winsome newcomer was somewhat smaller than Cutty but she was just as full of vigour and vitality for their joy at being together seemed to harness new wells of energy deep within the very core of their beings. Anna felt wonderfully happy again as the dolphins circled about her, never tiring of their frolics and games, the spray like silver wine dripping from their bodies when they hurled themselves high with such delicious abandonment. They were the happiest creatures in the world and Anna could not look at them without thinking that humans had a lot to learn from these giants — gentle giants that were imbued with all the mystique and magic of the deep unfathomed ocean.

Cutty seemed so proud, but was this his last farewell to her? the girl wondered. Had he come to say goodbye, to tell her he would be happy now that he had found a new friend amongst his own kind? Or would they both remain in the waters off Claddaheen? These were questions that had still to be answered but now they did not seem to matter for Anna must welcome Cutty home with a tune on the tin whistle. When she began to play he seemed to revel in those lilting notes, swimming and splashing with still greater animation and verve. Mella would be so thrilled when she heard the good news, Anna beamed, her father and mother and Caroline too and of course Donal and Tom. Now they would all have greater reason to rejoice when the film was previewed in the local cinema in a few days time and when Caroline's dolphin paintings went on show the same day.

Anna spent a great deal of time with the dolphins and it

was with great reluctance that she paddled back to the strand but her mother and father would be wondering where she was. How she envied Cutty and his mate for they did not have to go to school to do equations and fractions and geometry. She lingered on the strand, straining her gaze towards the frolicking dolphins. But if there was a hint of envy, there would always be admiration and love and longing too — a wild longing to be part of the wilderness they shared. She would have to think of a name for Cutty's new friend — or maybe she would give that honour to Mella. She took her bicycle and walked slowly up the grey ribbon of the road towards the main road above and beyond it to the farmhouse.

It was with renewed pleasure that Anna opened her dolphin diary again that evening for now there was much to write about: her father's eyes sparkling with joy when she told him of Cutty's return, Mella's tears, Donal's grins and yelps, Tom's smiles and Caroline's elated rush back to her cottage for her violin. Cutty deserved his happiness, her father had said, for he had given so much happiness to everyone who had seen him gambol in the water. Cutty was totally unselfish and how could anyone feel mean towards such a generous spirit? She had stood with her father on the strand, just the two of them together in the stillness of the evening, and he had placed his arm about her shoulder, making her feel warm and safe as he always did, and they had watched the dolphins without speaking, the glitter of the late September sun reflected in their eyes.

Anna paused and twiddled her pencil for a moment. She hoped, how she hoped, that Cutty and his mate would stay for a very long time in Claddaheen. If they did Cutty's companion might soon give birth to baby dolphins and that would be more wonderful still. But even if it were not to be she would be content just knowing that Cutty was not alone in the wild rolling swell of the sea. And in years to come she could sit by the crackling glow of the flames in the hearth and browse through her diary, rediscovering all the good times she had shared with Cutty, the wonderful wild dolphin of Claddaheen.